One Flower

A flower for her, only for her. Marion Warren bent down and crushed the red beauty to her face.

How long it had been since she had possessed something all her own! How she had tried to keep hope alive in the cold loneliness of the city!

Now a stranger had sent this flower. But who?

A thrill ran through her frail body. Perhaps fate had planned another meeting with the unknown young man she had encountered one evening in the rain . . .

Bantam Books by Grace Livingston Hill
Ask your bookseller for the books you have missed

Grace
Livingston
Hill

Crimson
Roses

*This low-priced Bantam Book
has been completely reset in a type face
designed for easy reading, and was printed
from new plates. It contains the complete
text of the original hard-cover edition.*
NOT ONE WORD HAS BEEN OMITTED.

CRIMSON ROSES

*A Bantam Book / published by arrangement with
Harper & Row, Publishers, Inc.*

PRINTING HISTORY

J. B. Lippincott edition published 1928

Bantam edition / December 1968

2nd printing ...... *January 1969*	6th printing .... *March 1971*
3rd printing .... *August 1969*	7th printing .... *February 1972*
4th printing .... *February 1970*	8th printing ...... *January 1976*
5th printing .... *June 1970*	9th printing .... *April 1981*

ISBN 0-553-14510-X

Published simultaneously in the United States and Canada

PRINTED IN THE UNITED STATES OF AMERICA

18 17 16 15 14 13 12 11 10 9

CRIMSON ROSES

Chapter I

THE ROOM WAS very still except for the ticking of the little clock, which stood on the table in the hall and seemed to Marion Warren to be tolling out the seconds one by one.

She sat by her father's bedside, where she had been all day, only rising to give him his medicine, or to tiptoe into the hall to answer some question of her sister-in-law's, or to speak to the doctor before he went out.

The doctor had been there three times since morning. He had come in the last time without being sent for. Marion felt sure that he knew the end was not far off although he had not definitely said so. As she looked at the gray shadows in the beloved face her own heart told her that her dear father had not much longer now to stay.

She would not call him back if she could to the suffering he had endured for the last two years. She knew he desired to be through with it. He had often spoken about how good it would be to feel that the suffering was all over. Yet she had hoped against hope that he might be cured and given back to her. She had nursed him so gladly, and loved her task, even when sometimes her head ached and her back ached and her slender arms ached, and her flesh fairly cried out for rest. Her father was almost her idol. He and she had always understood one another and had had the same dreams and ambitions. He had encouraged her in taking more time for reading and study than her more practical mother had thought wise. He had talked with her of life and what we were put on this earth to do. He had hunted out books to please and interest her. She had read aloud to him for hours at a time, and they had discussed what she read. And after her mother died he had

1

been both mother and father to her. How was she going to live without her father?

She had known, of course, since he was first taken ill, that there was a possibility that he might not get well. But he had been so cheery and hopeful always, never complaining, never taking it as a foregone conclusion that he was out of active life forever, and always saying at night:

"Well, daughter, I feel a little better to-night, I think. Perhaps the doctor will let me sit up in the morning. Wouldn't that be great?"

Yet he had also lived and talked as if he might always be going to heaven to-morrow. Once he had said:

"Well, I'm satisfied to live to be a very old man, if the Lord wills, or to go right now whenever He calls."

These memories went pacing before the thoughts of the girl like weird shadows as she sat waiting in the darkened room, watching the dear white face. She had had no sleep since the night before last when her father had grown suddenly so very much worse. At intervals she wondered whether she were not perhaps a little light-headed now.

Marion's brother Tom was sitting at the foot of the bed by the open hall door. He had been sitting there for an hour and a half. Occasionally he cleared his throat with a rasping sound. She knew he must be suffering of course, yet somehow she felt that she alone was the one that was being bereaved. Tom was older, and was not what he called "sentimental." He had never understood the deep attachment between Marion and her father. He sometimes had called it partiality, but the girl always knew her father had not been partial. He loved Tom deeply. Yet he had never been able to make a friend and comrade of his practical, cheery, and somewhat impatient son. The son never had time to read and talk with his father. He had always had some scheme on hand, to which he must rush off. He was like his bustling, practical mother, who even in her last illness had kept the details of the house and neighborhood in mind and sent others on continual errands to see this and that carried out as she planned. It was just a difference in temperament, perhaps. Marion wondered idly if Tom was thinking now how he might have made his father happier by being with him more. Tom loved their father, of course.

But Tom sat silently, dutifully, and now and then

changed his position, or cleared his throat. He seemed so self-possessed.

Marion was glad that he sat there. She would not have liked to have the responsibility alone. Tom had always been kind when it occurred to him. It did not always occur to him.

Jennie was there too, Tom's wife. She did not sit down but hovered in and out. Marion wished she would either go or stay. It somehow seemed like an interruption to have her so uneasy. It was just another thing to bear to hear her soft slipping around in felt slippers, calling Tom to the door to ask about some matter of household need, asking in that sepulchral whisper if there had been any change yet. Marion shuddered inwardly. It seemed somehow as if Jennie would be eager for the change to come. As if there were no sacredness to her in their father's dying. Yet that father had been exceedingly kind to Jennie. He had always treated her as if she were his own.

It was during one of these visits of Jennie to the sickroom that there seemed to come a change over the shadows on the white face. Jennie had breathed a syllable emphasizing it as it came, as some people will always make vocal a self-evident fact. Marion wanted to cry out: "Oh, keep still, won't you, *please!*" but she held her lips closed tight and drew a deeper breath, trying to pray for strength.

The doctor was coming in. They could hear the street door open and close softly. The latch had been left off that he might come in when he wished. Marion looked up with relief. Ah! The doctor! Now, if there was anything to do, it would be done!

The doctor noted the change instantly. Marion could understand by the grave look on his face that it was serious business. He stepped silently to the bedside, and laid practised fingers on the wasted wrist.

It was at that moment that the pale lips moved, and the eyelids opened, and her father looked at her.

Her hands were in his cold one instantly, and she thought she felt a faint pressure of the frail fingers.

"Bye, little girl!" he said faintly, "I have to leave you!" The eyelids closed, and she thought that he was gone, but he roused again and spoke in a clearer voice:

"You'll have your home here, Tom will see to all that. He'll understand——" The voice trailed off into silence.

3

Tom roused himself huskily and tried to speak, as if he were talking to one very far away:

"S'all right, Dad. I'll look after Marion. Don't you worry."

The sick man smiled.

"Of course!" he gasped, his breath nearly gone, "Good-bye!" His eyes searched the room.

"Jennie too, and the children!"

But Jennie had slipped away, suddenly.

Perhaps she was gone to her room to cry. Perhaps Jennie was fond of Father in her way after all, thought Marion.

But Jennie had not gone to cry. Jennie was stealing stealthily down the stairs, slipping like a wraith into the little den that had belonged to her father-in-law, where his big roll-top desk stood and his old desk chair, the walls lined with books. She closed the door carefully, snapped on the light and pulled down the shade, then looked furtively around. It was not the first time that Jennie had visited that room.

Since her father-in-law had been ill, and Marion closely held in his service, she had managed to make herself thoroughly familiar with every corner of the house. She was not going in search of something. She knew exactly what she was after.

She took out a key from her pocket and went over to the desk. The key had been in her pocket for a week. She had found it while putting away things in her father-in-law's closet. It had been on a key ring with other keys. She had taken it off of the ring one day when Marion was downstairs preparing some food for the invalid, while he was asleep.

Jennie opened the right-hand lower drawer of the desk and moved some account books over. Then she took out a tin box from the back end of the drawer. She fitted the key into the lock and opened the box. Breathlessly she turned over the neat envelopes carefully labelled "Deed of the House," "Tax Receipts," "Water Tax," and the like, till she came to the envelope labelled "My Will."

Jennie took this out, quickly put the rest back, locked the box, returned it to the drawer from which she had taken it, replaced the books, and closed the drawer. Then she picked up the envelope and held it in her hand for an

4

instant, an almost frightened look in her eyes, as if she were weighing the possibilities of what she was about to do. She did not open the envelope and read the will for she had already done that a week ago. Every word and syllable of the neatly written document was graven on her soul, and she had spent nights of waking, going over and over the brief paragraphs indignantly. The old man had no right to make a difference in his children. He had no right to leave the house entirely to Marion. If there *were* no will —that is, if no will were *found,* why the law would divide the property. Tom would look after Marion, of course, in any case. But Tom should have the right to decide things. He should not be hampered with a girl's whims. She could not see that what she was about to do was in any way wrong. No harm would come to her sister-in-law. In any case she would be cared for. It would simply smooth out things for Tom. And it was perfectly right.

Having shut her thin lips firmly over this decision she opened the upper right-hand drawer, pulled it entirely out, and laid it on the desk. Then she reached far in and laid the envelope containing the will carefully at the back of the opening, replacing the drawer and shutting it firmly again, even turning the key which was in the lock.

Having done this, she snapped out the light and groped her way to the door, unlocking it and stealing back into the hall. She listened an instant and then glided up the stairs as silently as she had come down, a nervous satisfaction in her face.

She appeared in the doorway an instant too late to hear the last kindly word from her father-in-law. The doctor had raised his head from bending over to watch, and Marion was turning away with her hands to her throat and a look of exalted sorrow on her face. Marion was so queer! Why didn't she cry? Jennie began to cry. It was hardly decent not to cry, Jennie thought. And Marion pretended to think so much of her father! Probably, though, she was worn out and really glad it was over. It was perfectly natural for a girl not to enjoy taking care of an old sick man for so long. Two years! It had been two years since Father took sick! Well it was over, thank goodness, at last! Jennie buried her face in her handkerchief and sobbed gently. Marion wished again that she would keep still. These last minutes, and the precious spirit just taken its flight! It seemed a desecration!

The doctor and Tom were talking in low tones in the hall now, and Marion turned back for one last precious look. But even that look had to be interrupted by Jennie, who came with an air of doing her duty and stood at the other side of the bed.

"Poor old soul! He's at rest at last!" she said with a sniff and a dab at her eyes with her handkerchief. "And you, Marion, you haven't any call to blame yourself for anything. You certainly have been faithful!" This by way of offering sympathy.

It was piously said, but somehow the unwonted praise from her sister-in-law grated on her just now. It was as if she were putting it in to exonerate herself as well.

"Oh, please, please keep still!" shouted Marion's soul silently. But Marion's lips answered nothing. She still wore that exalted look. After all, what did anything like this matter now? Let Jennie voice her meaningless patter. She need not pay attention. She was trying to follow the flight of the dear spirit who had gone from her. She had not yet faced the life without him that was to be hers now that he was gone. She still had the feeling upon her that for his sake she must be brave and quiet. She must not desecrate the place by even a tear.

All through the trying days that followed until the worn-out body was laid to rest beside the partner of his youth in the peaceful cemetery outside the city, Marion had to endure the constant attentions of her sister-in-law. Jennie was always bringing her a cup of tea, and begging her to lie down. Jennie wanted to know if she wouldn't like her to come into her room and sleep lest she would be lonely. Jennie slapped the children for making a noise and told them their Aunt Marion didn't feel well. Jennie became almost effusive in her vigilance until after the funeral was over. Marion was glad beyond words to be allowed at last to go to her own room alone and lock the door. To be alone with her sorrow seemed the greatest luxury that could now be given her.

And while she knelt beside her bed in the room that had been hers during her father's illness because it was next to his, and she could leave the door open and listen

6

for his call in the night, her brother Tom was down in the den going over his father's papers.

Tom was a big pleasant-faced man with an easy-going nature. He would not for the world hurt anybody, much less his own sister. He intended with all his heart to take care of her all her life if that was her need and her desire. He had not a thought otherwise. Yet when he began the search among those papers of his father it could not be denied that he hoped that matters were so left that he would have full charge of the property without any complications. He had certain plans in the back of his head that an untrammelled will would greatly facilitate. He and Jennie had often talked about these plans, and Jennie had urged him to speak to his father about it some day while there was time. But Tom did not like to seem interested; and, too, there was something about his father, perhaps a kind of dignity that he did not understand, that made Tom embarrassed at the thought of broaching the subject of money. So Tom had never said a word to his father about the property.

Once or twice Tom's father had dropped a word to the effect that if anything happened to him, Tom was to look after his sister, and Tom had always agreed, but there had never been anything definite spoken regarding the house, or what money was left, or even the life insurance. And Tom had never broken through the silence.

During that last afternoon when he had sat in the sickroom, tilted back against the wall in the shadows, clearing his throat now and then, he had been thinking about this. He had been wondering if for all their sakes he ought not to try and rouse his father and find out just what he had done, how he had left things. But Marion had stayed so close to the bedside, and somehow he could not bring himself to speak about it with Marion there. There was something about Marion's attitude that forbade any such thing.

But after his father had spoken to them about the house and about Marion, and said that he would understand, Tom had been uneasy. Perhaps after all his father had complicated things by putting Marion into the will in such a way that he would have continually to ask her advice and get her to sign papers and be always consulting her. He hoped against hope that his father had not been so foolish. Poor father! He had always been so visionary. That

7

was the word Tom could remember hearing his mother call his father, visionary. She had said once that if father hadn't been so visionary they might all have been rich by this time, and Tom had decided then and there that he would profit by his father's mistakes and not be visionary.

But although Tom was a little worried, and thought about it quite often, he would not open the desk nor try to find out anything about matters until his father was laid to rest. It did not seem fitting and right. Tom had his own ideas of what was the decent thing to do.

He waited until his sister had gone to her room and had had time to get to sleep, too, before he went to the den. It wasn't in the least necessary for Marion to have to worry about business. She was a woman. To his way of thinking women should not be bothered about business affairs, they only complicated matters. He always tried to make Jennie understand that, too. Sometimes he talked things over with her, of course, as she was his wife, but when it came to the actual business he felt that he was the head of the family.

So he had told Jennie to go to bed, as he had some papers to look over and might not go up for an hour or so yet, and he betook himself to the father's desk, armed with his father's keys.

But Jennie was not so easily put off as Tom thought. Jennie crept to her bed with an anxious heart. She had put the little key back on the bunch with the other keys and felt that no one in the world would ever find out that she had had it, but yet she could not sleep. She could not help lying there and listening for Tom.

Jennie did not feel that she had done anything actually wrong. Of course not, her queer little conscience told her briskly. Why, she might easily have destroyed that will and nobody been any the wiser. But Jennie felt most virtuous that she had not. Of course she would not do a thing like that! It would have been a crime in a way, even though its destruction was a good thing for all concerned. But to put it away carefully was another thing. The will was there. It was like giving Providence one more chance to save the day. If anything ever came up to make it necessary it could be found of course. Why worry about it? It was safely and innocently lying where there was

8

little likelihood of its ever being found, at least not till long after everything had been satisfactorily settled. And Marion wouldn't make a fuss after a thing was done anyway. Suppose, for instance, Tom sold the old house and put the money into another one out in the country. Jennie loved the country. But Marion was queer sometimes. She took strong attachments and one of them was this old house. She might make a lot of trouble when Tom tried to sell it if she owned it outright, as that will made her do. It was perfect idiocy for Father ever to have done that anyway. It wasn't right for a man to make a distinction between his children, and when he did it he ought to be overruled.

So Jennie lay awake two hours until Tom came to bed, wondering, anxious, and beginning to be really troubled about what she had done. Suppose Tom should somehow find it out! She would never hear the last of it. Tom was so almost overconscientious! Well—but of course he wouldn't find it out!

And then Tom came tiptoeing in and knocked over a book that had been left on the bedside table, and Jennie pretended to wake up and ask what he had been doing. She yawned and tried to act indifferent but her hands and feet were like ice and she felt that her voice was not natural.

Tom, however, did not notice. He was too much engrossed in his own affairs.

"You awake, Jennie? Queer thing! I've been looking through Dad's papers and I can't find a sign of a will. I was sure he made one. He always spoke as if he had."

"Mmmmm!" mumbled Jennie sleepily. "Will that make any trouble? Can't you get hold of the property?"

"Oh, yes, get the property all right. Sort of makes things easier. The law divides things equally. But of course I'll look after the whole thing in any event. Marion doesn't know anything about business. Gosh, I didn't know it was so late! Let's get to sleep. I'm dead tired. Got a hard day to-morrow, too!" and Tom turned over and was soon sound asleep.

Chapter II

"THIS HOUSE OUGHT to have a thorough cleaning," announced Jennie coming downstairs a few days after the funeral. "It hasn't been cleaned right since Father has been sick. I couldn't really do it alone, and of course I knew you couldn't spare the time to help. Suppose we get at it this morning. It'll do you good to pull out of the glooms and get to work."

Marion reflected in her heart that it was not exactly lack of work from which she had been suffering, but she assented readily enough. She had not been able to do much housework for the last five years, and it probably had been hard on Jennie. So she put on an old dress and went meekly to work, washing windows vigorously, going through closets and drawers and trunks, putting away and giving away things of her father and mother. That was hard work. It took the strength right out of her to feel that these material things, which had belonged to them and been as it were a part of them, were useless now. They would never need them any more.

Of course most of her mother's things had long ago been disposed of, but there were her father's clothes, and the special things that had belonged to his dear invalidism. It was hard to put them away forever. Yet Jennie demanded that they be sent to a hospital.

"That bed table and the electric fan and the little electric heater and the hotwater heater. They give me the creeps to look at them. It isn't good to have such reminders around, Marion. You want to get away from everything that belonged to the sickroom. I for one want to forget sickness and death for a while and have a little good time living."

10

Marion felt that Jennie was a bit heartless in the way she talked about it, but she realized that it would be better to put the things where they would be doing someone some good, so she packed them tenderly away and sent them to a poor little new hospital, in which her church was interested, and sighed as she took down the soft curtains from the invalid's windows and washed the windows and set them wide, realizing that the sunshine would not hurt tired eyes in that room any more, and could be let in freely without hindrance.

"Would you mind if Tom and I were to take Father's room now?" asked Jennie the next day. "Then Bobby and the baby could have the room you've been occupying and you can go back to the room you used to have before we came. It would change things around a little and not seem so gloomy in the house, don't you think?"

The house didn't seem gloomy to Marion the way it was, and she felt it rather sudden to tear up her father's room and give it to another use, but of course it was sensible and better in every way for the children to be next to their father and mother. So she said she didn't mind, and they set to work moving furniture and changing things from one closet to another.

And after all, Marion rather enjoyed getting back to her old sunny room at the back of the house, with the bay window her father had built for her, her own little bookcase full of books, and her own pretty furniture her father and she had picked out years before. It brought sweet and tender memories and made her feel that life was a little more tolerable now. She could retire to her own pleasant room and try to feel like her little-girl self again, lonely and sad, of course, but still at home in the room that her father had made for her just after her mother had died, the sunniest, prettiest room in the house, she felt. It was a wonder that Jennie didn't like it. Still, of course, she wanted to have the children nearer, and where they had been sleeping in the guest room was too far away for comfort. Now Nannie could come down from the small, third-story room and take the room the children had been occupying. It was better all around. But yet, she felt a lingering wistfulness about that front room where the invalid had lain so long. It was hard to feel its door shut, and to know it did not belong to her anymore.

11

It seemed as if Jennie was so anxious to wipe out all memory of her father.

But Jennie gave Marion very little time to meditate over these things. She seemed restlessly eager to keep something going all the time. At breakfast one morning she said to Marion:

"Marion, I don't see why you don't get out and see your friends now. There's nothing to hinder. Have a little company in and make the place lively. It will do you good. It's been so gloomy all the time Father was sick. Let's have some life now. Don't you want to ask some friends in to dinner or lunch or something?"

Marion roused from her sad thoughts to smile:

"Why, I guess not, Jennie. I don't know who I'd ask I'm sure. Nearly all my old school friends are married or gone away or interested in their own affairs. I really haven't seen any of them for so long they would think it queer if I hunted them out now. I never did go out much you know. When I was in school I was too busy, and after Mother got sick I had no time."

"Well, you're too young to get that way. You'll be an old maid before you know it. Tom, don't you think Marion ought to get out more?"

"Why, if she wants to," said Tom good-naturedly. "Marion always was kind of quiet."

"Now, Tom, that's no way to talk. You know Marion ought to get out among young folks and have good times. She's been mewed up too long."

But the tears suddenly came into Marion's eyes and her lip quivered:

"Don't, please, Jennie!" she protested. "I wasn't mewed up. I loved to be with Father."

"Oh, of course," said Jennie sharply, "we all know you were a good daughter and all that. You certainly deserve a lot of praise. But you owe it to yourself to go out more now. It isn't right. Shut up in a city house. If only we lived out in the country now it would be different."

Marion didn't quite see why the country would be any better but she tried to answer pleasantly:

"Well, Jennie, I am going back and take my old Sunday School class if they still need me. I had thought of that."

"Oh, a Sunday School class!" sniffed Jennie. "Well, if that pleases you, of course. But I should think you'd want to get in with ṣome nice young folks again. My land! This house is as silent as the tomb! Why, I had lots of friends in Port Harris before we came here to be with you. They would run in every day, and we'd telephone a lot in between. They do that in the country or in a small town. But in a city nobody comes near you. They aren't friendly."

"I suppose you are lonely, Jennie," said Marion apologetically. "I hadn't realized it, I have been so occupied ever since you came."

"Oh, I'm never lonely," said Jennie, tossing her head. "I'm thinking of you. I could be alone with my house and my children from morning to night and never mind it. It's you I'm worrying about."

Marion looked at her sister-in-law in mild surprise. It was so new for Jennie to care what became of her. Jennie had manifested very little interest in her during the years she had been living with them. What had got into Jennie?

When they came to clean the den Jennie insisted upon doing it herself, saying she thought it would be too hard for Marion yet awhile, it would remind her of her father too much. Marion tried to protest, but when she got up the next morning she found that Jennie had arisen before her and finished cleaning the room entirely, so that there was nothing left for Marion to do in there. She stood for a moment looking around on the bare room with its book-lined walls, its desk and worn old chair, and the little upholstered chair where she used to sit by her father's side and study her lessons in the dear old days when he was well and she was still in school. Then she dropped into the desk chair with her head down on the desk, and cried for a minute.

A wish came into her heart that she might have her house to herself for a little while. Just a little while. Of course it was nice of Jennie to be willing to come there and do the work all these years while there had been sickness. Of course Jennie had given up things to come. She had come away off from her own father and mother who lived up in Vermont, and she had not liked the city very well. But oh, if she just wouldn't take things into her own hands quite so much and try to make her sister do everything she thought she ought. If she only hadn't come into this sacred room and done the cleaning! It seemed to Marion that the spirit of the room had been hurt by such unsympathetic touches as Jennie would have given.

But that was silly of course! So Marion raised her head and wiped her eyes and summoned a smile to go out and help Nannie wash the breakfast dishes, but somehow day after day the strange, hurt feeling grew in her heart, that all the precious things of her soul life were being commonized by Jennie, yet Jennie was doing it out of kindness to her. If only there were some way to let Jennie know without hurting her feelings. Marion was gentle and shy and couldn't bear to hurt people's feelings.

Then Marion began to think about what Jennie had said. Perhaps she ought to get out more. Perhaps she ought to hunt up her old friends.

So she went to church the next Sabbath. She had always loved to go to church, but it had been so long since she had been able to leave her father and go, that it seemed strange now to her to be sitting alone in the old seat where she and Father had sat.

She had dreaded this and had even ventured to suggest to Tom that perhaps he would go with her. Jennie had declined most decidedly. She couldn't leave the baby. But Tom said he had to see a man who had some property for sale and he wanted to find out about it. So she had to come alone.

But it was good to be there again, after all, in spite of the loneliness, and she had a feeling that her father would be pleased she had gone.

The minister came down and spoke to her kindly. He asked if she wouldn't come back and take her old Sunday School class again. One of the ladies came over and asked her if she wouldn't come out to the Mite Society social and help wait on the folks, they had so much trouble getting girls to come and be waitresses.

Marion agreed to come although she shrank tremendously from it. But it was something she could do, of course, and she felt she ought not to refuse. Jennie was most enthusiastic about it and offered to go with her, but

14

when the evening came Jennie had a cold and so she had to go alone.

As she entered the big Sunday School room where the social was to be held she had an instant of hesitation. It seemed to her she could not go through a long evening all alone with strangers. She had always been a shy girl, and her five years of service caring for Mother and then Father had made her still more so. She was at home among books, not humans. If her books could have come alive and been present at that gathering, how gladly would she have walked in and conversed with their characters, one by one, thrilled by the thought of meeting those she knew so well. But a lot of people frightened her. She liked to be on the outside of things and watch. She loved to weave stories to herself about people, but to have to move among them and make conversation was terrible. She had purposely come late to avoid having to sit and talk a long while with someone while people were gathering.

But a group of merry girls was coming in behind her and she hated to have them stare at her, so she hurried in and took off her coat and hat in the ladies' parlor which was already well decorated with hats and wraps.

The bevy of eager girls entered just as she turned to go out, shouting and laughing, gay in bright-colored dresses, combing their bobbed locks, some of them even dabbing on lipstick, holding up their tiny hand mirrors and chaffing one another loudly in a new kind of slang which Marion did not in the least understand. They were very young girls, of course, but some of the things they were saying were shocking. Could it be that girls, nice girls, girls who belonged to the church and Sunday School talked like that nowadays?

She shrank away from them and went into the main room.

For a moment she was dazed before the babel of tongues and the medley of gay dresses. Someone was playing the piano and everybody seemed trying to talk as loud as possible to be heard above it. She felt somehow a stranger and an alien.

She began to look about for someone she knew.

Off at the other side of the room were a group of young people, three of them old schoolmates of Marion's. Mechanically she made her way toward them, half hoping they might welcome her to their midst. There was Isabel Cresson. She used to help Isabel with her algebra and geometry problems in school. She had never been especially intimate with her, but at least she was not a stranger.

But when she arrived at the corner where the young people had established themselves she was not met with cordiality. Anna Reese and Betty Bryson bowed to her, but Isabel Cresson only stared.

"Oh, why you're Marion Warren, aren't you?" she said with a condescending lift of her eyebrows. "How are you? It's ages since I've seen you. I thought you must have moved away."

Marion tried to explain that her father had been ill and she had not been able to be out, but Isabel was not listening. She had merely swept Marion with a disconcerting glance which made her suddenly aware that her dress was out of date, and her shoes were shabby, and then turned her eyes back to the young men with whom she had been talking when Marion arrived.

Marion mechanically finished her sentence about her father's recent death, feeling most uncomfortable and wishing she had not explained at all. Isabel turned her glance back toward her long enough to say, "Oh, too bad. I'm sorry, I'm sure," and then got up and moved across to the other side of the circle to speak to one of the young men. She did not excuse herself nor say she would be back. She did not suggest introducing Marion to the young men. No one made any attempt to move or include her in their circle. She dropped down in a chair just behind them, too hurt and bewildered to get herself away from them immediately.

The girls and men chattered on for some minutes ignoring her utterly. Once she heard Isabel say with a light laugh in response to something one of the men had said:

"Yes, one meets so many common people at a church affair, don't you think? I've coaxed Uncle Rad to let us go to some more exclusive church out in a suburb you know, or uptown, but he doesn't see it. He was born and brought up in this church and nothing will do but we've all got to come. I've struck, however. I simply can't stand the affairs they have here constantly. I only came tonight because I was asked to sing. Say Ed, did you hear that Jefferson Lyman is home? That's another reason I

16

came. They say he is coming here to-night just for old times' sake. I don't much believe it but I took the chance."

"And who is Jefferson Lyman?" asked the young man who was evidently a newcomer in town.

"Oh, mercy, don't you know Jeff? Why he's an old sweetheart of mine. We used to be crazy about each other when we were kids. Walked back and forth to school together and all that. Jeff's been abroad for five or six years, and they say he's tremendously sophisticated. I'm just dying to see him."

"But who is he? Does he live around here? Not one of *the* Lymans, from the Lyman firm?"

"Sure, boy!" said Isabel. "He's the Lyman himself, all there is left. Didn't you know it? His father and his uncle are both dead. That's why he's come home. He's to be the head of the firm now. He's young, too, for such a position. But he's been abroad a lot. That makes a difference. I'm simply crazy to see him and renew our acquaintance. Yes, he went abroad for the war, of course, was in aviation, won a lot of medals and things; and then he stayed over there, looking after the firm's interests part of the time, travelling and studying. He's a great bookworm, you know. But he's stunningly handsome, if he hasn't changed, and he's no end rich. My soul! He owns the whole business and it's been going ever since the ark, hasn't it? He's got a house in town right on the avenue with a picture gallery in it; that house next the Masonic Club, yes, that's it, and an estate out beyond the township line on a hillside where you can see for miles, and a whole flock of automobiles, and an army of servants, and a seashore place up in New England with a wonderful garden right out on the beach almost, among the rocks. Oh, it's perfectly darling. We motored past it last summer on our trip. I'd adore to live in it!"

"Gracious!" said Betty Bryson. "If he's got all that why does he come to a church social? I'm sure I wouldn't bother to if I had all that."

"Well, perhaps he won't come," said Isabel. "I'm sure I wouldn't either. But they say he's interested in the church because his father helped to found it, and he always comes when he's home and there's anything unusual going on. You know this is the minister's twenty-fifth anniversary, and there's just a chance he may come. I should

17

think he'd be disillusioned, though, wouldn't you? All these common people. Why some of them aren't even dressed up decently!" and Isabel lowered her voice and cast a covert glance about. Marion somehow felt she was looking at her. She rose suddenly and made her swift way toward the kitchen. She would look up the woman who had asked her to come and say she would have to go home, she was not feeling well or something. She simply could not go around among those dressed-up girls. She would drop something, surely, feeling like this. Oh, why had she been led to come to a scene like this? Why did they have things of this sort anyway? There was no worship in it, and what else could people want of it? How terrible those girls had been. Cruel and terrible. And Isabel Cresson, how she had changed and coarsened. Her lips and cheeks were painted. What a difference it made in her. She used to be a pretty girl with lovely golden curly hair, and now it was all cut off, close, like a boy's. That might be pretty on some people, perhaps, but Isabel looked too big and old for it.

Marion's pale cheeks were flushed now, and her tired eyes bright with distress. She had never had quite such an experience as this, being turned down by an old schoolmate. One who had been under obligation to her, too, in the old days. What was the trouble? Wasn't she dressed right?

She glanced down at her plain brown dress, made in the fashion of two years ago. It was still fresh and good, but of course the fashion was behind the times. Why hadn't she realized that she needed to furbish up her wardrobe before going out into the world? She must attend to that before she went anywhere, even to church again. But what kind of people were they all to look down on an old acquaintance just because she was oddly dressed? She had been shut away from the world so long that she had got far away from the sense of worldliness. How odd it was that just dress made so much difference. And what a silly she was. Was she going to cry right there in the church before all those people? Oh, Jennie and Tom had been all wrong! She was not fit to go out anywhere. She was all tired out and needed to stay at home and rest and just be quiet.

She was edging her way through the merry crowds

toward the church kitchen now, hoping to make her excuses and get away, when the minister loomed in her way and greeted her with a royal smile, and his wife put a comforting arm around her and began talking in a low tone saying dear things about her father; telling her just how she had felt when her father was taken away. The tight lines of suffering around Marion's delicate lips relaxed a little and she began to look almost happy. Then with a swoop Mrs. Shuttle, the chairman of the entertainment committee arrived:

"Well, here you are at last, Marion Warren!" she exclaimed in a loud voice that made Marion shrink. "We've been looking all over the place for you. We want you terribly in the kitchen right away. The woman we hired to wash dishes hasn't come yet. She's always late nowadays. She's got a little baby and can't leave early, and we find the Christian Endeavor used the glasses and ice cream plates at their last social and just left them in the closet dirty! Isn't that the limit? Something ought to be done about that. And see, we're almost ready to serve and not enough ice-cream plates nor glasses. You wouldn't mind washing a few for us would you, Marion? I told them I thought you wouldn't. We're almost wild back there in the kitchen. Come on!"

So Marion vanished into the kitchen and was presently established at the church sink washing dishes. Of course she could wash dishes. She had done that all her life. It was much less embarrassing than being out there in the other room being made to feel as if she came out of the ark. Yes, she was glad to wash dishes. She would rather wash dishes than serve. Much! Oh, much! This was what she said when it was discovered that the woman with the little baby did not arrive at all, and that many more dishes beside the glasses and ice-cream plates would have to be washed before the evening was over.

So Marion stayed in the kitchen and washed dishes the rest of the evening, and rejoiced that she was not called upon to go back into the big room and be looked at. Never, never, never would she come to anything again till she made sure she was dressed just right! And never would she come at all just for pleasure.

Marion did not even eat any ice cream. The thought of it was revolting to her. She felt cold and hot and wanted to cry, but she washed dishes faithfully all the evening and smiled when each new tray full was landed on the table beside her, and did not groan nor complain, and was rewarded at the end by commendation from Mrs. Shuttle.

"Oh, Marion, you've been just wonderful! I can't thank you enough! You love to wash dishes, don't you? You make dish washing a fine art, don't you? Now, you really do! I wish you would come every time and help us. We'll remember you when we get in a strait again."

"It's a small thing to do," said Marion trying not to let her voice sound weary.

"And will you really come and help us again?"

"Why, surely," said Marion, "if you need me," and resolved if she did, that she would enter by the back door and not go at all into the main room. It was all well enough to serve the Lord in the church by washing dishes if she was needed, but there was no law at all either moral or spiritual to compel her to force herself on the church socially. She would never do it again.

So Marion went home at half past eleven, having wiped and set up the last hundred glasses and spoons herself, and let herself in at the front door with her latch key, and hoped that Jennie had gone to bed.

But Jennie was very much awake. She called down from the head of the stairs:

"Mercy! What kept you so late? Did you have a good time? You must have, to stay so long. Did anyone come home with you?"

"I was washing dishes," said Marion wearily. "No, I didn't have an especially good time. I stayed because the dishes had to be washed. No, no one came home with me. The janitor offered to, but I told him it wasn't necessary."

"Well, I certainly wouldn't have stayed," said Jennie indignantly. "What do they think you are? A servant? I wouldn't go to that church any more if I were you. There are other churches. Anyway, perhaps we're not going to stay here much longer. Tom's heard of a farm for sale up in New England. He's taking the New York express tomorrow at six. We'll have to get breakfast by five. You better get right up to bed or you won't wake up. I can't be depended on to do much, you know, because the baby is sure to wake up and yell."

Marion stood in the hall where she had been when Jennie called to her and stared at the pattern of the wall paper dazedly as she heard Jennie shut her door with a click and snap off her light. So that was the next thing that she was going to be confronted by, was it? They were going to try to go away! They were wanting to sell the house and go away from the only spot on earth that was dear to her!

She went over and sat down on the lower step of the stairs and put her face down in her hands and thought how tired and sick she was of it all, and how wonderful it would be if she could just slip away and go where her father had gone.

After a few minutes she got up sadly, locked the front door, turned out the light and went up to her room. After taking off her hat and coat she dropped upon her knees by her bed, and let her heart cry out to God.

"Oh, God! What am I going to do? How am I going to bear it? Won't you take care of me?"

Praying thus she fell asleep upon her knees, and woke hours later, stiff and chilly, to creep under the covers shivering and so to sleep again, with a dull, vague realization that she must get up pretty soon and get breakfast for Tom.

Chapter III

THE LIGHT HAD BEEN turned out in the kitchen to save electricity while they ate supper, and Marion Warren did not turn it on when she slipped away from the table with her hands full of dishes. She did not wish to have anyone see the trouble in her face. By the light that came through the open door she scraped the dishes quietly and filled her dish-pans without much noise, that she might hear what her brother was saying.

Tom Warren was a large man with heavy movements and a voice to correspond. His sister had no difficulty in hearing it above the subdued clatter of the dishes.

He had arrived home but an hour before from the trip to Vermont, whither he had gone to look at a farm that was for sale at a low price. The days of his absence had been a time of anxiety for his sister, and of eager expectations for his wife. Jennie was hovering about him now, interrupting him occasionally with a chirp of assent as she helped to clear off the table. She resembled a sparrow whose mate has just brought home a new twig for the nest.

Tom talked on in his large, complacent voice. He was immensely pleased with his "find." The farm was all and more than it had professed to be. The house was in good repair, the location charming and healthful, the land rich and under a good degree of cultivation, with a convenient market for its produce. He had all but said that he would take it.

"A grand place for the babies to play," he said. "No one will have to stop work to cart them out into the street for the air. No brick walls, no dust, no noise. You and Marion will have nothing to interrupt you from morning till night. The nearest neighbor is half a mile away, and it's two miles to the village. That needn't bother us any; we'll have a car, of course, and when the children get old enough to go to school, Marion here can teach them all they need to know. She's always been crazy to teach. How about that, Marion?" raising his voice unnecessarily. "It isn't every family that has a schoolmarm all ready-made."

But Marion did not answer. The gentle clatter of the spoons in the dish-pan might have drowned his question. He did not stop to see.

The girl in the darkened kitchen caught her breath in a half-sobbing sigh, and the tears came into her eyes; but she kept her peace and went on with her task.

"I'm going to see Matthews in the morning," went on Tom joyously. "If he sticks to his offer about buying this house, I'll accept it and bind the bargain for the farm to-morrow. Then how soon do you two ladies think you can get ready to move? If Matthews buys this house, he's likely to want possession at once."

Marion gasped, and drew her hands from the dish-water suddenly. She hesitated for an instant, then appeared like a wraith at the dining-room door, her wet hands clasped, her delicate face looking ghastly white against the dark background of the kitchen.

"Tom!" she said in an agonized voice, "Tom!"

Tom wheeled about his chair and faced her, startled from his contented planning.

"Tom! You're not going to sell this house! The house that Father worked so hard to buy and to pay off the mortgage! Our home! My—my home! Tom, you know what Father said."

The last words were almost a cry of distress.

Tom frowned uneasily. Jennie's face grew red with anger.

"That's just like you, Marion Warren!" she burst out hotly. "Three little children that you profess to love, your own nephews and niece, languishing in the crowded city air, and needing the lovely country and a chance to play on the green grass, and you letting a mere sentimental fancy for a little old house stand in the way of their life, perhaps!"

Jennie's eyes flashed sparks of steel as gray eyes can do

23

sometimes. Marion shrank from their glance, her very soul quivering with their misunderstanding of her.

"O, now, Marion," began Tom's smooth tones, "that's all bosh about Father's slaving to pay for this house. Sentimental bosh," he added, catching at his wife's adjective. "He worked hard, of course. All men with a family do. I work hard myself. But you know perfectly well that Father wouldn't have hung on to this particular house just because he had worked hard to pay for it, if he had a good chance to better himself. It isn't throwing it away to change it into something better, and this is a great opportunity. As for its being your home, why, you'll have a home with us wherever we go; so you needn't get up any such foolish ideas as that. The farm'll be your home as much as this is in three months' time. Don't be a fool."

He said it kindly in his elder-brother way; but Marion's face grew whiter, and she stood looking at him as if she could not believe what he had said. Her great dark eyes made him uncomfortable. He turned from her, and went to wind the clock.

"Come, hurry up, Jennie," he said with a yawn. "Let's get to sleep. I'm about played out. It's been a hard day, and I must get up early in the morning to catch Matthews before he goes to the store."

Marion dropped silently back into the kitchen, and finished her dishes. Jennie came in presently, and turned on the light with an energetic click, looking suspiciously at the silent figure wringing out the dish-towels; but Marion's face was turned from her, and she could not see whether or not there were traces of tears upon it. Marion hung up the dish-towels on the little rack beside the range and went silently upstairs.

Jennie listened until she heard the door of Marion's room close; then she went back to her husband.

"Do you think she'll make trouble about selling this house?" she asked anxiously.

"Trouble? Pooh! She'll not make trouble," he said in his complacent voice that always soothed his wife. "She'll have her little cry over giving it up, but she'll be all right in the morning."

"But doesn't she own half of it?" queried the wife sharply. "Hasn't she a right by law to object?"

"Yes, she owns half of it but she'll never object. Why,

she'd give me her head if I told her she ought to," said the husband, laughing.

"She might give you her head," said Jennie with a toss of her own; "but she's got a terrible will of her own sometimes, and I've an idea she's got it on the brain to go to normal school, yet."

"Nonsense!" said her husband, ponderously. "She's too old! Why, she's almost twenty-three."

"Well, you'll see!"

"Well, *you'll* see. I guess my sister has some sense! Come let's shut up shop."

Marion locked her bedroom door, and went straight to her white bed, kneeling beside it and burying her face in the pillow.

"O Father, Father," she whispered, "what shall I do? How can I bear it?"

Long after the house was silent she knelt there trying to think. By and by she crept over to her back window, and, sitting in her willow chair, rested her cheek against the window-frame. The spring air stole in and fanned her cheeks, and blew the tendrils of damp hair away from her temples soothingly, like a tender hand.

The Warren home was a pleasant red-brick house with white marble trimmings and marble steps. It was in a nice, respectable neighborhood, with plain, well-to-do neighbors, and neat back yards meeting on a cement-paved alleyway. In a few weeks now these back yards would be carpeted with well-kept turf and borders of gay flowers. Her own crocuses and hyacinths and daffodils that her beloved father had taught her to care for were even now beginning to peep through the earth. Her window had always framed for her a pleasant world of sights and sounds that were comfortable and prosperous. She loved to watch and compare the growing things in the green back yards, or to enjoy their clean white coverings in winter; and she knew every varying phase of cloud or clearness in the bit of sky overhead. She looked up now, a broken moon beamed kindly down between dark, tattered clouds.

Within, the room was a white haven of rest. The simple enamel bed with brass trimmings, the white bureau and wash-stand, the willow chair, the plain muslin curtains, and the gray rugs with pink borders had all been the gift of her loving father. They represented sacrifice and extra night-work after the wearisome day's toil was completed, and some had been acquired under protest of the more practical mother, who felt that the money might have been displayed to better advantage in the parlor.

Marion loved her white room. It seemed an inner shrine to fortify her soul against the trials and disappointments of life. And the bit of window view of flying cloud and neat yards and brick rows was a part of it all. The whole was linked eternally with precious memories of her dear father. And her brother was planning to take them all away! It was appalling!

It was not that she did not appreciate pure air and green grass and unlimited sky. She, more than the rest of the family, had the artist eye to see the beauties of nature. But the change meant to her a giving up of her life-ambitions, a cutting herself off from the great world of education. Ever since her childhood she had longed for a fine education and contact with the world of art and culture. She and her father had planned that she should be a teacher, and to that end she had taken great care with all her studies. Her mother had felt that she had had quite enough of school when she was graduated from the high school, but her father encouraged her to take up the normal course. But five long years of nursing had broken in upon her fondest hopes. She realized that it was rather late for her to think of going back to the normal school and completing her course. Quietly, patiently, she had relinquished the idea. Nevertheless, she had hoped to be able to do something else in the world that would bring her into contact with the things she most longed to see and hear and know. And the city was the only place where she could hope for that.

There were lectures, free libraries, great music, and sometimes exhibitions of wonderful pictures. She felt instinctively that there was still opportunity for her to acquire a certain amount of true education and mental culture; and she knew in her inmost soul that it was not to be found in that Vermont farmhouse, where the days would follow one another in a monotonous succession of homely household duties, enlivened by Jennie's pleasant shallow chatter. Jennie's idea of life was to keep one's house speckless, and then to sit down with her sewing in

26

the afternoon and enjoy it. She could not understand what more Marion wanted.

That might be all very well for Jennie. It would be Jennie's house and Jennie's children. Jennie cared for no more. It was certainly commendable in her. She was a good wife and mother. But Marion, even though she owned a part of the house, could not seem to feel that she really belonged there, since her father's death. It was as though the home had passed into other hands.

Jennie had taken command in the house years ago, when Marion's mother first fell ill, and had always treated Marion as if she were a child who ought to do whatever she was told. There had been nothing else to do at that time, but to put Jennie in command. It had been good of Jennie to be willing to give up her own home and come to help them out. Marion had always recognized that, and tried patiently to do whatever Jennie asked in the ceaseless round of duties, relieving Jennie whenever it had been possible. But now she felt that the time had come when she could no longer go on as an under-servant, stifling the life that was in her for no reason at all. If it had been necessary for Tom's sake, or even for Jennie's or for the children's good, in any way, she would never have faltered. But there was no reason for anyone's sake why it was necessary for her to go on working in her brother's household, almost as if she were a sort of dependent. Half of the property, of course, belonged to her. And Tom had been doing a good business. He had money in the bank aside from what his father had left. If Tom went to farming he would make that pay, too. He was a stirring, successful man. He could afford to hire a servant if Jennie wanted one. And Nannie was old enough to help a good deal. She often cared for the baby when her mother was busy.

Of course, if they had stayed on here at the old home, Marion would have felt that for a time, while the baby was so young, she ought to give all the help she could to Jennie. But Jennie seemed to talk as if this state of things was to go on forever. Marion knew now that it could not. It must not.

When Tom had first heard of the farm in Vermont and began to talk about going to see it, Marion had hoped against hope that the farm would not please him. But now, as she lay awake through the long night and thought it all out, she knew that she had been sure all the time that Tom would want to sell this house and buy that farm. And she knew that back in her consciousness she had been just as sure then as she was now that she was never going to be willing to go to Vermont with them. She felt it would be like being smothered both mentally and spiritually, out in the country away from all opportunities, with no books save the few she owned, no lectures or courses of study open to her, few chance meetings with helpful people, not even a church within walking distance. Marion's church life, quiet and unobtrusive though it had been, was very dear to her, the church of her father and mother, the church of her childhood. The prospect looked utterly dreary to her. And yet, if she refused, what was she to do? Demand her part of the money and buy another house, a smaller one? And try to keep house all by herself? That would be dreary, lonely, but peaceful perhaps. But Tom would not be able to purchase his farm, unless he had all the money that came from the sale of this house, and Tom would be bitter about it. Jennie would, anyway. Jennie's people lived in New England. She had always longed to go back.

For the first time since her father's death Marion considered seriously the matter of her inheritance.

Tom had said there was no will, and seemed to consider that it meant that they had all things in common. That might be all very well while they remained in the old home, but if they separated what ought she to do about it? Demand her share? Of course her father had intended that she should have her part. Almost his last words had been about the home. Poor Father, he would not have liked Tom to sell the house. He had loved it as much as she did. But surely she had some right in things. What ought she to do about it?

She had willingly signed all the papers Tom had brought to her at the time the estate was settled up, and asked no questions. She had been too sorrowful to care. Tom would, of course, do the right thing. Naturally, Tom would be terribly upset if she asked for money. He wanted to put everything into that farm. Also, he would think that Marion ought to stay with them and be taken care of. She did not like to stand in the way of his desires. Perhaps if she made no trouble about the sale of the house, if she quietly gave up her share he would the more readily agree to her staying in the city. In fact, after her long vigil she began to see clearly that if she could not bring herself to go with the family to the country, it was plainly her duty to give up her share of the property. This was not, of course according to her father's plan for her, but it seemed the only way without coming to an open clash with Jennie, and hurting her brother irretrievably. If she gave up her claim, surely there was nothing left for Tom to say. She had a right to live her own life and do the things her father had planned for her to do.

Of course, she reflected, it would be a great deal harder to accomplish anything in the way of education without money. She would have to earn her living, and that would leave little time for study. But there would be a way. She was sure there would be a way for her to be independent. It was the only thing possible. It would be equivalent to mental and spiritual death to live her life out with Jennie. They had not a thought in common. She must get out and away and breathe the free air. She must live out some of the longings of her soul or she would die of stagnation. Life was not merely a round of household duties spiced with gossip and blame. Why Tom and Jennie scarcely ever even went to church. Sunday was like every other day to them, a day to get more done. They wondered at her that she cared to waste her time in teaching a Sunday School class, and why she was interested in a church that brought her no social life.

If they had stayed in the dear old home where all her precious memories clung she might have endured it, but since they were going to a strange place it was far better she should leave them. And she was conscience-free, surely, if she gave up her share of the property. If Father had left a will, it would have been different, perhaps, but since he had not done so, it was better to say nothing about it. Just let it all go. There would be some way. She would not ask for a penny.

Marion came down early the next morning and got breakfast. There were dark rings under her eyes and her lips were white; but otherwise she wore the same quiet calm that had been on her face during the patient years of serving her mother and her father.

Jennie eyed her sharply and drew a breath of relief that there was no sign of rebellion on the sweet sad face.

Tom came in with his boisterous good-morning and appeared to have forgotten all about the little outbreak of the night before. He ate his breakfast hastily and hurried off to find Matthews.

Marion washed the breakfast dishes as usual. Jennie was impatient with her that she did not talk. It seemed sullen and ugly of her. Jennie wanted to bubble over about the prospect of the farm, and was annoyed that she could not. She did not understand Marion's attitude of quiet resignation. Jennie had never cared for red brick with marble trimmings. She had lived in a suburb before she was married, and had ideas about a single house and a Dutch hall; but a Vermont farmhouse might have possibilities of spaciousness beyond even a Dutch hall.

Tom came home at noon in high glee. Matthews had paid a hundred dollars down to bind the bargain. He was to pay the remainder in ten days, and wanted possession at the end of the month.

Marion said nothing, but wore a white, pained look as if she had braced herself to receive this blow and would not wince. Jennie and Tom stole furtive glances at her, but made no reference to her words of the evening before.

Marion ate but little lunch and hurried through the dishes afterward. Jennie watched her uncertainly. At last she said:

"Marion, what if you and I take down the curtains and wash them this afternoon. We can't begin too soon to get packed. A month isn't long."

"I'm sorry," said Marion gently, as she washed her hands and hung up her apron, "but I have to go out this afternoon. I'll try to help to-morrow morning."

Then she went up to her room leaving Jennie vexed and mystified and worried. What in the world could Marion have to go out for? Why did she have to be so terribly close mouthed? She was acting very strange indeed, Jennie decided. Maybe she was going to make trouble after all. Tom was always so cocksure about everything. He ought to have had a good talk with his sister and let her get her grouch out of her system. This silent gentleness was dangerous.

She watched behind the parlor curtains and saw Marion

signal a trolley going downtown, and went back to her work with uneasiness. She wished Tom would come back. He ought to know Marion had gone out.

Half an hour later Marion entered the imposing building of a great trust company down in the city and timidly approached the clerk behind the steel-grated window, frightened at her own temerity, so that her voice fluttered as she asked for the president of the great concern.

"Mr. Radnor is very busy to-day," said the brusque young clerk eyeing her doubtfully, noting her shyness and shabbiness, and growing haughtier. "He has a meeting of the board of directors at three o'clock and it is a quarter to three now. I doubt if he can see you this afternoon."

"Oh," said Marion with a quick little movement of her hand to her fluttering throat, "Oh, I won't keep him but a moment. If you would just tell him my name, and ask him if I can see him just for a word—it won't take long."

The clerk hesitated, but wrote down her name and gave it to a messenger, who departed through a great mahogany door into the inner regions. Marion stood palpitating. Now, if he shouldn't be able to see her to-day she would have to come again, and there was so little time! Each day counted for a lot. And when Jennie got started at tearing up the house it would be next to impossible to get away without explaining, and that would be fatal to her intentions. She felt her only chance for success was to keep her plans to herself until they had matured. Tom would surely find some way to frustrate them unless she did.

But suddenly the messenger returned through the heavy door, and nodded to the clerk, who turned with a more respectful look, and informed Marion that Mr. Radnor would see her for a moment if she would be brief.

Now it happened that the president of the trust company, who was also superintendent of Marion's Sunday School, and senior elder in the church to which she belonged, had known and respected Marion's father for a good many years, and was also a kindly soul. So when Marion, fairly frightened out of her senses, to think that she had dared to come into such an august presence, was presently ushered into his inner sanctum, he greeted her with great cordiality and seated her in one of his big leather chairs.

"Good afternoon, Miss Marion," he said beaming pleasantly upon her. He prided himself that he knew the entire Sunday School by name, and never made a mistake although there were some fifteen hundred on the roll. "I am glad to see you, although I have but a few minutes to spare before a most important meeting. Is there anything that I can do for you? Your father was a man whom I greatly honored, and whose friendship I prized beyond most. He was a man of God if there ever was one."

Marion looked up with a sudden light in her eyes and forgot her fright.

"And he had a great admiration for you, Mr. Radnor," she said shyly. "He once said he would rather ask a favor of you than of any man he knew, because he said you treated a poor man as if he was a prince."

"Well, he was a prince if there ever was one," said the bank president heartily, "and I feel honored that he so honored me. Now, if there is any service I can render his daughter I shall be doubly pleased."

"Well," said Marion, with a sudden return of her embarrassment, "I want to get a position as a saleswoman in a department store. Could you give me a letter of introduction somewhere to someone you know? I think I could be a salesgirl. It seems to me the work would be easy to learn, and I would try with all my ability to do credit to whatever recommendation you feel you can give me."

"Why, surely," beamed Mr. Radnor heartily.

He delighted to do favors to members of his Sunday School, and it happened that this request was one that he was peculiarly able to grant just at that time. One of the chiefs in a great department store was under heavy obligation to him. He felt reasonably sure that anything he asked of the man at that time would be readily granted. Moreover, he was one who delighted to please others, especially when it cost him little trouble. He turned to his telephone and called up his man.

Marion's cheeks glowed with pleasure as she listened to the one-sided conversation and heard the glowing praise of her father's sterling character and the kindly words about herself. In wonder she listened, and knew the gate of her desire had swung wide at the magic touch of this great man's word.

It was just one minute of three when the bank president hung up the receiver and turned to Marion graciously smiling.

"It is all right, Miss Marion" he said in the same tone he used to announce the annual Sunday School picnic, "you can have a position as soon as you are ready to take it, I think. You'll need to answer a few questions, of course, but they are mere formalities. Mr. Chapman has promised to give you something worthwhile. You had better go right over and make out the application blanks while it is fresh in his mind. He said he could see you in half an hour. You are to come to the second-floor office and inquire for Mr. Chapman. Here, I'll give you my card"; and he hastily wrote across the top of his card, "Introducing Miss Marion Warren," and handed it to her.

"Don't think of thanking me. No trouble whatever. I'm only too glad that it was possible for me to do it. It is fortunate that you caught me just at this time as I am usually out of the office before this hour. Now I must go to my appointment. Sorry I can't visit with you a few minutes. I hope you'll have no trouble in securing just what you want at a good salary. He promised me he would do his best for you financially for a start and give you opportunity to rise. Come back if you have any trouble but I don't think you will. Good-afternoon. So glad you came."

It was over, the dreaded interview.

Marion stood on the steps of the great building and looked back at it with awe as an employee lazily closed and fastened the great gate of shining steel bars. The massive stone building seemed to tower kindly above her as if it had been a kind of church in which some holy ordinance had been observed, so truly she felt that God had been kind to her and helped her in her need.

Chapter IV

SHE HURRIED TO THE department store, full of tremors. As in a dream, she passed through the ordeal there. She came out a half hour later dazed with the rapidity of the machinery through which she had passed. She went to the waiting-room, and sat down for a minute or two to think it over and steady herself. She dared not go home to her sister-in-law with the strangeness of it all upon her. It seemed queer to her that people passing back and forth in the store did not look at her and see from her eyes that something unusual had happened to her. She was engaged, regularly engaged, as a saleswoman, although it had been strongly impressed upon her that the size of the salary she was receiving was entirely due to the influence of the bank president and that, in the words of the brusque Mr. Chapman, it was "up to her" to get more pay as rapidly as she chose. It was at the ribbon-counter that she was to begin, but perhaps some day she might attain to the book department. Mr. Chapman had intimated that there might be a vacancy there soon, and he would see. Her eyes shone in anticipation. To handle books! To know them as if they were people, acquaintances! To be among them all day long! What joy that would be!

She sat quietly thinking it over for at least ten minutes, looking around on the great store with its rising galleries and vaulted arches; listening to the heavenly music that came from the organ up in the heights somewhere among those tiers of white and gold pillars. It was her store. She was part of it. In a little while she was to be one of the wheels in the great mechanism that made this institution possible. She would be where she could watch the multitude of passing faces, hear the grand music, and now and then catch passing bits of uplifting conversation. It was wonderful, wonderful! How glad her father would have been! Of course he would have been sorry, grieved, that it must be just as a salesgirl she was to start out in life, and not as a teacher; but that could not be, and she knew he would have been glad of this opportunity for her.

Then, with a little quaking in her heart at the thought of Tom and Jennie and what they would say, she rose hurriedly and wended her way through the store; a little frail figure of a girl, with shining eyes and a flower face, her plain, neat, street suit and black felt hat attracting little attention beside the gaudy spring attire that flaunted itself on every hand.

She had to stand in the trolley car nearly all the way home; for it was after five o'clock, and cross, tired shoppers filled up every seat before the shy girl could reach them. The red had faded from her cheeks by the time she reached home, and Jennie noticed that she looked worn and tired, albeit the glow in the girl's eyes puzzled her.

"Where on earth have you been?" she questioned sharply. "I should think with all there is to do you might have hurried home."

"I have been to see someone," said Marion as she had planned to say. "I came home as soon as I could."

"H'm!" said her sister-in-law significantly. "Well, I've taken down all the curtains and washed them this afternoon, and I'm tired; so you can get supper. You better hurry, for Tom has to go out this evening early."

Without answering, Marion laid aside her hat and coat, and obediently went into the kitchen, tying on her apron as she went. In spite of her she could not get rid of a feeling of guilt in the presence of her sister-in-law, but out in the kitchen by herself she felt like singing at the thought of the prospect before her. She would not have to take orders from Jennie any more, nor bear her frowns and sharp words. She would be her own mistress. There might be orders in the store, of course there would, but she would have her hours, and her times when she might do as she pleased. Her whole life would not be under unsympathetic surveillance.

But Jennie was not nearly as unconcerned as she tried to appear. She was genuinely worried. Had Marion somehow found that will? Did she suspect that it had been hidden? She longed to go to the old desk and see whether it was still where she had hidden it, but she did not dare lest Marion should see her and suspect something.

"Do you suppose she's been to see a lawyer about whether she's got to sign away her part of the house?" questioned Jennie in a whisper when Tom came home.

"Nonsense! Jennie," exclaimed her husband, "what's got into you? Marion won't make a fuss. She never did in her life. She's a meek little thing. She wouldn't dare. You'll find her as interested in the plans as you are in a few days."

"Well, I'm not so sure," said his wife with set lips. "I shall breathe easier when that deed is signed."

"Fiddlesticks!" said her husband. "You leave Marion to me, and for pity's sake don't talk to her about it. Half the trouble in this world is made by this continual haranguing. Women always have to yammer a lot about everything. It makes a man sick!"

Nevertheless at the dinner table he eyed his sister surreptitiously and seemed anxious to conciliate her. He talked a lot in a loud breezy tone, and tried to make them all laugh. He laughed a great deal himself, and spoke of what nice times they were going to have on the farm. He passed Marion the cake twice, instead of eating the last piece himself as he usually did.

"How about it, girls?" he asked jovially as he carefully picked up some crumbs on the tablecloth beside his plate. "Can we get packed up in three weeks?"

"Of course!" said Jennie sharply, not daring to look at Marion.

"How about it, Marion, do you think we can?" asked her brother, as Marion arose to clear off the table.

"Why, I should think so," said Marion coolly as she gathered up a stack of dishes.

She felt as if she were shouting it, and marvelled how willing she was now to have the house sold, if sold it must be, since she had a new life before her. Not that she was at all reconciled to leaving her home, but she had decided that it was the right thing to do to let Tom get his farm, and having decided, she had put it away from her thoughts. She knew the wrench was going to be very great when it came, but she did not feel quite so bitter about it, now that she had a prospect of something besides the desolation of a farm life in Jennie's continual company.

But she did not want her brother to discover her secret yet, so she hurried out of the room lest he suspect something in her acquiescence to his plans. She knew that the traditions of the family made it imperative that she should be taken care of. Tom was old-fashioned. He would not think it right to leave her alone in the city. He would feel he was not doing his duty by her. Tom was determined to do right by her, though his ideas of what were right for her were sometimes out of focus.

She had not yet planned how to carry out the rest of the project, nor how to break the news to her brother that she was not going with him to Vermont. But if he found it out too soon he would surely manage to upset all her plans, and perhaps make it necessary for her to go after all.

But Tom was not of a suspicious nature, and was too conceited to think that his sister would stand out long against him. So he only raised his eyebrows at his wife with a knowing "See, Jennie?" and began to whistle.

After that the packing went merrily forward, and no one could complain that Marion did not do her share, though all the time her heart was exceedingly sorrowful at leaving her old home.

When Wednesday evening came, Marion hurried through the dishes, and put on her coat and hat.

"Marion, you're never going to prayer meeting to-night after the way you've worked today!" exclaimed Jennie disapprovingly. "I think you owe it to us to stay at home and rest, if you won't consider your own feelings. There's more yet to do to-morrow. You ought to stay at home and go to bed."

Marion turned in dismay at this new obstacle to her plans. She had been troubled to seem to dissemble about the prayer meeting, but it was the only way to get a chance to go out and hunt a boarding-place without being questioned, and a whole week was gone already. She looked at her sister-in-law in distress.

"I would rather go, Jennie," she said, and felt as if she were uttering a lie. "You know I am used to going out Wednesday night—"

"Well there's such a thing as carrying religion too far

and making it ridiculous. You're going away from here soon now, anyway, and it doesn't matter one prayer meeting more or less. From now on I think you'll be plenty busy without prancing off to that church where the folks don't care a straw about you, anyway. Besides, if you have any strength left, I wish you'd stay home and help me let down Nannie's dress for travelling. She's grown so tall it won't do at all."

Marion stood uncertainly by the door. Was it possible she must stay at home this evening? Just then help arose from an unexpected source.

"Oh, let her go if she wants to, Jennie. She always was a great one for church, and we're going off in the country where she can't get to church often. She might as well take her fill before we leave. As for letting down Nannie's dress, I'd wait till I got there, for she'll have trouble in going on a half-fare ticket if you make her look a day older. Run along, Marion; you've earned your evening. Do as you like with it."

Marion cast a grateful look at her brother, and hurried out into the darkness, still feeling guilty with the knowledge that she was not going to church to-night, yet afraid to say anything lest she should be stopped.

Tom retired behind his paper, while his wife informed him that he made a perfect little goose out of Marion. No wonder she was spoiled. If he was half as good to his wife, he'd have kept his sister at home to help her this evening. She was too tired to put the children to bed.

Whereupon he informed her dryly that Marion was nearly twenty-three years old, and didn't have to do as she was told, in fact, didn't have to live with them at all; so he didn't exactly see the point. After which he folded up his paper and put the children to bed himself, which process mollified his wife somewhat, but also gave him a period in which to reflect on the usefulness of unmarried sisters.

Marion's evening was a fruitless search. She could not find anywhere in the neighborhood a room that was not far beyond her pocketbook. And it began to seem as if boarding houses, at least any that looked at all possible, were only for multimillionaires.

Marion felt that her disappointment was a just reward for staying away from prayer meeting, and she went home more downcast than she had been since her brother announced his intention of selling the house. How could she find a place to live without explaining the whole matter to her brother? Perhaps that would yet be the only way out of her difficulty. But now to her uncertainty was added the fear that there were no places where she could possibly afford to live that would not be intolerable for one reason or another. They were either too hot or too cold, or too unsanitary, or too utterly distasteful in some way, when they were not too expensive. Once in a while she would find one that she thought could be made to do, and then she would discover some terrible drawback, and have to move on to another place. So she came home a trifle later than she usually came from prayer meeting, and had to meet Jennie's sharp eyes and prying questions about why she was so late.

Two days later, however, Jennie announced her intention of taking the baby and making a flying farewell visit to her sister, who lived in a small town thirty miles away. She would go early Friday morning and return Monday. She felt that the packing was well started and Marion could do a good deal while she was gone. Marion's attitude had been so pleasant and willing that her fears were somewhat set at rest, and she longed to have a little ease herself, for she had worked very hard. She knew, too, that Marion could pretty well be counted on to do the work of two people in her absence, so she went with a mind free to enjoy her holiday.

Marion had agreed to the suggestion readily enough. She knew she could work early and late and still have time free for what she wanted to do for herself, and Jennie's absence seemed really providential. Tom was away all day from breakfast until evening settling up his business affairs, not even coming home to lunch on Friday or Saturday he said, so she was free to do as she pleased.

So Marion hurried through the breakfast dishes and locked the door on the duties Jennie had suggested, and took her way down town to hunt a place to live.

She had several plans. There was a girl who used to be in the same Sunday School class who worked down town, a stenographer or something. She boarded somewhere. She would go and ask her some questions.

But the girl was very busy taking dictation and could not be seen for a long time, and when she did appear she gave very little help. Yes, she boarded not far from her office, but it was rotten board, she said, and not a very pleasant bunch of boarders. She was thinking of making a change herself. Lots of girls took a room and got their meals at restaurants, or did some cooking in their rooms, but she couldn't see that after working all day. She suggested several places where Marion might look for rooms, and Marion finally went away armed with addresses, much wiser and more anxious.

She longed inexpressibly for a room of her own, no matter how tiny it might be. The idea of a small gas stove appealed to her tremendously. Even without a gas stove she felt sure she could manage her breakfasts, and perhaps an occasional evening meal. Or, if she took a good meal at a restaurant in the middle of the day she might make her evening meal, usually very simple, milk and fruit and crackers or cereal, and that could be managed in her own room of course. She disliked the thought of constant daily contact with other boarders, especially since her talk with this other girl who made it plain what kind of people she had to mingle with in a cheap boarding house. A restaurant was different. One did not have to be so intimate with a crowd as with individuals at the same table.

She went to one of the restaurants the girl had suggested and ordered a glass of milk and some crackers, and while she was eating them studied the menu. It seemed from the card to be quite easy to select a substantial meal for a very small sum if one was careful about counting the cost. If the lack of variety palled she could always try another restaurant.

Before the morning was over she had gone into many dreary little dark halls, and climbed many steep narrow flights of stairs in her search, till she began to feel that nowhere in the wide world was her little refuge to be found at any price which she could hope to pay, and her promised wages which at first had seemed so large began to dwindle. How very little it was going to be able to purchase in the way of comfort for her. Oh, if her father had foreseen this, how troubled he would have been! Perhaps she was doing wrong. Perhaps she ought to go with Tom.

But no, she had her own life to live, and her father would have been just as disappointed to have had her lose the other things of life, which were only to be had if she remained near the city with its music and art and libraries and evening schools. She must have a chance.

Now and then a feeling of a sob came in her throat. It ought not to be so hard for her. She ought to have her part of what her father had left. But she shrank inexpressibly from Tom's look when he told her as he surely would, that she was spoiling all his prospects in life by her silly whims, and that of course, if she wanted her half of the money it would be impossible for him to get the land he wanted, but together they could have a nice home. No, let him have the home and be satisfied. She would take her chance without the money. Then he had nothing for which to blame her.

So she toiled on fom apartment house to apartment house, in fruitless search.

About the middle of the afternoon, and just as she was beginning to think with sinking heart that she would have to take a little hall bedroom without heat or give up her plan entirely, she came at last upon a room that seemed to have possibilities.

It was on the third floor back in the saddest of all the sad little houses she visited, and its roof sloped at the sides.

It had no heat, but there were two lovely dormer windows looking toward the river, and the spring was coming on. She need not think of heat. Besides, the sad-faced woman who took lodgers said there was a pipe-hole in the chimney, and she had an old wood-stove that she wouldn't mind putting up in winter if the young lady would bring up her own wood. Seeing the young lady had her own furniture, and wouldn't even require a carpet, she would let her have it very cheap.

Marion joyfully accepted the proposition. The landlady had reluctantly agreed that she might move her things in as soon as was convenient, but the rent was not to begin until the first of the month, which was a little more than a week off.

All the way home the girl was trying to think what

41

would be best to do about moving her things. She knew her brother would make serious objection to her remaining in the city. He might even go so far as to refuse to let her take her things out of the house. Not that he had any right, of course, for the things were her own; but she knew he would use any method to prevent her staying if he took the whim to be obstinate about it. Marion felt she could afford to run no risks now. She must get her furniture moved at once, and then keep her door locked. There was no other way.

As soon as dinner was out of the way she shut herself into her room, and went to work. Tom had gone out again as soon as he finished his dinner, so she was not hindered by anything, and he had not thought to ask her what she had been doing all day. Her eyes were bright with excitement and unshed tears. But she had no time to cry. Tenderly and hurriedly she took down the few pictures and little ornaments, and packed them into the bureau drawers with as many of her other belongings as she could get in. She packed the china wash-bowl and pitcher carefully, wrapping them in an old quilt, and tied newspapers about the white bed and other furniture until the room resembled a ghostly edition of itself.

When all was done, she lay down upon the bare mattress, her head upon the tied-up pillows, and her raincoat spread over her. She was not sure how she was going to sleep the rest of the nights they stayed in the house, but she was too tired to care. She meant to get her own things into her own little room before her brother and sister-in-law found out anything about it. After they were once safely out of the house she could work with a free mind.

She carried out her purpose the next morning, securing a wagon to take her furniture, and then hurrying in the trolley car to her new quarters to receive her things and see them safely housed. The landlady had had the room swept and the floor wiped up. The spring sunshine was flooding the windows, and all together Marion felt that it was not a bad prospect for a home.

As soon as the furniture was all carried in she locked the door, and sped back to her neglected work. The rest of the day she worked as if her life depended on getting things done, not even stopping to get any luncheon for herself. She had paid the first month's rent and the mover out of her own small hoard, which had been saved from time to time during many years. She had but fifteen dollars left on which to live until she should receive her first week's pay, but she felt confident she could make it do, and she was happy in a way, happier than she had been since the death of her father.

She hurriedly improvised a temporary bed for herself from the old cot used during her father's illness, stored away in the loft. Then, taking care to lock her door, she went at the duties that her sister-in-law had suggested she should do.

It was not until Tuesday morning that Jennie discovered the locked door.

Chapter V

IT WAS THE AFTERNOON before the goods were to be
taken away. Marion had been hoping against hope that
she could keep her secret until a few loads had left the
house. Then surely no one would notice her room was
practically empty, or think anything of it. She had suggested to Jennie that it would be a good time for her to go
to the stores for a few last things that she needed for the
journey and that she herself would stay and direct the
men what to take first. It seemed as if everything were
going all right for the furtherance of her plans. But she had
not calculated on the whims of her sister-in-law.

Marion was in the kitchen packing pots and pans, salt
cellars and kitchen cutlery, labelling each box carefully
so that those who unpacked it would have no trouble in
finding everything. Suddenly Jennie appeared in the doorway with her eyes blazing angrily and a sneer on her tired,
dirty face.

"Marion, what on earth do you keep your door locked
all the time for? You act as if you expected us to steal
something!"

Marion turned and tried to smile in the face of Jennie's fury.

"Why, it looked so untidy up there. All my things are
spread out you know. I started to pack my clothes this
morning."

If only she could keep Jennie in good humor so that
Tom would not have to know yet!

"Well you certainly are a prude if there ever was one.
Give me the key. I want to go in there and throw these
pillows and a rug out of your window. It will save lugging
them downstairs."

44

Marion turned, wondering what to do.

"Why, let me go up and throw them down," she said pleasantly. "Here, you sit down in this chair and finish wrapping these little things. You look tired to death."

But Jennie turned on her almost in a fury:

"Give me that key!" she said. "I believe you are afraid I'll pry into your things, or maybe take something. But I'm not standing anything more from you, and I haven't time to argue. Where is the key?"

"Jennie!" said Marion in distress, "you know that isn't true. I just thought it would rest you to sit down a while."

"Oh, yes, *rest!*" sniffed Jennie. "I haven't time for rest. And I hate doing that little finicky work anyway. Finish what you've begun and give me the key."

Marion with set lips and cheeks turned suddenly scarlet handed over the key and went on with her work. Perhaps the revelation might as well come this way as any other. It was bound to be hard any way.

"How queer you look at me," said Jennie as she grabbed the key. "I actually believe you don't want me to go into your room."

Jennie hurried upstairs and Marion could hear her dragging the heavy rug to the door, fitting in the key and unlocking it. There was an instant's silence—ominous silence, and then, angry footsteps hurried down the stairs and Jennie burst into the kitchen again:

"What on earth does all this mean?" screamed Jennie, her eyes fairly snapping. "I knew you were up to some tricks you were so meek and quiet. And now I see why you locked your door. People don't keep locked doors in their own house unless they have something they're ashamed of to hide. What have you done with your furniture, Marion Warren?"

Marion turned around and faced her angry sister-in-law, her face white but calm, her voice as gentle as her state of nervous excitement would admit:

"Listen, Jennie, it was my own furniture. I had a right to do what I liked with it. I have done nothing I am ashamed of."

"No, I don't suppose you are ashamed. You don't know enough to know when you ought to be ashamed. Well, what have you done with it? Sold it? Because if you have I'm sure I don't know where you're going to get any more

45

to furnish your room. Are you intending to sleep on a cot all your life and keep your hairbrush and comb on the floor?"

"No, I haven't sold it, Jennie," said Marion trying to steady the involuntary tremble that would creep into her voice. It always made her tremble to face Jennie in one of her fits of anger.

"Well, what have you done with it? For mercy's sake don't waste all the afternoon telling me. I'd be glad to know the worst at once."

"It isn't dreadful, Jennie," said Marion looking at her wistfully. "I really think perhaps it will be a relief to you in the end. I've sent it away to a room I've hired."

"A room you've hired! Indeed! And what have you hired a room for I'd like to know?"

"To live in," answered Marion simply.

"To live in!" screamed Jennie. "You don't say! And who is going to support you while you live in it, may I ask? Or is that a secret? Perhaps that's something you'd like to hide behind locked doors, too!"

There was a covert sneer in Jennie's words that brought the vivid color to Marion's cheeks sweeping up over her brow, and then receding again leaving it white as death. Her eyes, too, had grown cold with hurt dignity.

"I have taken a position in Ward's store," she said almost haughtily, and turned back to her work again, trying to down the stinging tears which threatened.

The angry sister-in-law stood speechless for a moment too taken aback for words. At last she spoke, biting words that stung as they fell about the troubled girl.

"And you call that right, do you? You think you're a Christian, don't you? You're always going to church and prayer meeting and pretending to be better than anybody else, and you're always so hypocritically sweet and patient. Oh, yes, but you're sly! The idea of your going to work and sneaking your furniture out of the house as if you thought we might steal it, and going about it in an underhanded way, just to make your brother trouble. Here he's slaving and planning to make a nice permanent home for you, where you will be cared for all your life and be safe and comfortable, and you act up like this! Why didn't you come out straight and tell him you didn't like him? Answer me that! Why didn't you tell him all about it?

There must be some hidden reason why you want to stay. You're afraid to tell your brother. I understand."

Jennie was so angry now that she did not really know what she was saying.

"There's probably some man at the bottom of this. There's always a man!"

But suddenly Marion turned and took hold of her furiously, her face white, her eyes black with indignation. She took hold of Jennie and shook her.

"You shall not say a thing like that! You shall not! It is not true, and you know it is not true! I could not go to Vermont. My father wanted me to stay here and get an education! I couldn't go away! You have no right to say such things about me!"

Marion had caught Jennie unaware and for a moment had been able to punctuate her sentences by shaking her as if she had been a child too astonished to recover herself. But her slender hold had not a chance in the world against Jennie's stout arms, and in a moment more Jennie had wrenched herself free and dealt a resounding slap on Marion's white cheek.

Stinging with pain and humiliation Marion buried her face in her hands, and moaning turned and fled up to her room, blindly stumbling over the heavy rug which Jennie had left in a heap in the doorway. Falling headlong, she lay for a moment, too crushed to do anything but lie there shaking with silent sobs.

Then suddenly she realized that she must not let herself be defeated this way. She had done wrong perhaps to shake her sister-in-law, even though she had insulted her, but she was in the right in demanding her freedom. She must go down and face Jennie again and explain.

Hastily dashing the tears away she got up and went downstairs to the furious Jennie:

"Jennie, I am sorry I shook you," said she gently, "although you said something that made me very, very angry."

"Oh, yes, you're sorry now," flashed Jennie gloating over Marion's humiliation. "You're afraid of what your brother will say, laying hands on his wife. It doesn't look very well for a Christian to go around shaking people just because she doesn't like to hear them tell her the truth and call a spade a spade, but you'll have to learn that

47

the world won't stand for your sly ways, and Tom won't either. Well, as far as I'm concerned, I'm glad it came out for once. Tom always thinks you are so sweet and meek and gentle. I wonder what he'll think now. The idea of attempting to shake me! Tell me what I shall say and what I shan't. You sly little minx—you. Get out of my sight! You make me sick, getting up a scene like this and planning to upset all your brother's plans.

"Jennie, that isn't true," said Marion boldly. "It can't possibly make any difference to you whether I go to Vermont or not, and I have not done anything wrong, either. I have only taken away the furniture which my father gave me when I was a little girl. I have not even asked for my share of the money from this house, or from my father's life insurance, or from his other property, although I'm sure I must have had a perfect right to do so. I thought it over and decided that I did not want to have Tom disappointed about the farm he meant to buy, and I could not see why it should make any difference to either of you if I stayed behind, so long as I gave up my share of the property."

"Property! Property!" babbled Jennie too angry to reason,"as if property were everything. As if of course, the property wouldn't be a man's to look after. As if your father didn't expect you would stay with your brother and behave yourself like a decent girl, and not try to run around alone and set up a bachelor establishment like these common flappers! As if you weren't leaving me with all the work of settling and the children to care for and everything, and me off alone there on the farm without any company or anyone to relieve me day in and day out!" She raged on but Marion had control of herself now.

"Listen! Jennie, you didn't have to go on a farm if you didn't want to, and you had no right to demand that I go, anyway. Tom is perfectly able to hire help for you if you want it!"

"Yes, hire, hire, hire help! As if Tom was made of money! You're perfectly willing your brother should go to a great expense while you lie around and have a fine time!"

"Jennie! Stop! I'm not going to lie around and have a good time. I'm going to work hard and earn my living and get more education. And at least you will have the price of my board and keep extra, if you don't count that I had any right in my father's property. You don't seem to realize that you have taken away the home that I love from me. My father always said——"

But Jennie, with a frightened look at Marion, had fled to her room and locked the door behind her, and Marion could hear her sobbing aloud for a long time.

Marion feeling that she had made a mess of everything and disgraced her Christian profession as well by losing her temper, went around finishing the rest of her work with sorrowful heart and troubled eyes in which were many unshed tears.

She tried to get together a nice little supper with the few utensils that were not packed, but when Tom came in the storm was all to do over again, and nobody attempted to eat anything until it was all cold. Jennie came down to meet her husband in a perfect torrent of angry tears, as soon as she heard his step in the house, and Marion had the added sorrow of seeing her brother turn horrified unbelieving eyes in her direction, and reprove her bitterly:

"Marion! I never thought this of you. Is that really true? Did you lay hands on my wife and shake her?"

Marion opened her white lips to protest, but no words came from her parched throat. She could only stare at her brother with wretched eyes. How could she speak up and say that Jennie had slapped her in the face? How tell that they had come to a common low-down fight, like two fish-wives, she a Christian, and her brother's wife! How justify herself? And because her heart was almost broken that Tom, her brother, should believe all that and not know that there was something to be said in her defence, she could not speak. Her throat refused her breath to clear herself.

So she had to stand there speechless and hear Jennie tell the whole miserable story over in her own version, blaming her and never telling what she herself had done.

And finally she had to see her brother soothing his wife, and petting her clumsily, and telling her she was all worn out, and that she must go upstairs and lie down and he would bring her some supper, she needed to rest, and then he helped her up the stairs, with cold reproachful looks at Marion who had caused all this trouble.

After a long, long time, Tom came down and harshly called to her.

"Now, Marion, let me hear what you have to say. What is all this nonsense about you hiring a room? Of course you know I can't permit it."

Marion stood up straight and slim, and white to the lips and tried to say the things she had planned to say to her brother, but her lips trembled so she almost broke down.

"Tom, I'm not a little girl. I'm of age. You have no right to say 'permit' to me. I have a right to stay here where Father planned that I should stay. And I am not doing wrong. I have deliberately planned to give up whatever share of the property I should have had and to earn my own living——"

"So you think I'm so mercenary, do you, that all I will care will be about the property?" he interrupted, the hard, cold look in his eyes.

"Oh, Tom!" cried Marion. "Why won't you understand?"

"No I can't understand," he said coldly. "This is merely a streak of stubbornness in you and I suppose I shall have to let you go and try it before you will believe what a fool you are making of yourself. Everyone knows that Father was visionary——!"

"Tom!" cried Marion. "Don't! Don't!"

"No, I won't," said Tom, "because it is of no earthly use. You have that streak in you and I suppose you can't help it. It will have to be taken out of you, and I guess it won't take long working for your living, before you find out. Very well, go your own gait, and learn your lesson to your sorrow. You are of age, of course, and I can't prevent you forcibly. You've got the bug of education in your head, and you don't realize that you're too old now to make anything out of that. You've got all the education any reasonable woman, who is decent and stays in her own respectable home, needs. But you've got to find it out, so stay, and learn your lesson. But remember, that when you've learned it, your brother is ready to forgive you and take you back. There'll be a nice comfortable home waiting for you with plenty of all that any woman needs to make her happy. You don't see it now, but the time will come when you'll be sorry and ashamed that you have treated your only brother this way. And you don't think for a minute, do you, that Father would want you to desert us and live by yourself in the city? Answer me that?"

"Tom, I think he would," said Marion sorrowfully. "The last thing he said was that I would have a home here in this house."

"Oh, you're going to harp on that again, are you? You are trying to punish me for selling this house. Well, you should have said so before it was sold. It is too late now. You had a perfect right not to sign your name to the deed if you didn't want to, but you never even mentioned ——"

"Tom, I begged you that first night——"

"Oh, yes, I know you went into hysterics at first. I expected that. But after you knew all the story, about what a wonderful place we were getting——"

"Well, Tom, I haven't blamed you about the house, I only——"

"Oh, yes, you have blamed me. You said that Father said you were to have this house and I had taken it away from you. You as much as said that. Come now, didn't you?"

"Tom, if you twist what I said that way I can't talk any more about it. I——"

"Very well, young lady, don't talk! I won't talk either! No, I don't want to hear any more of your explanations. They are all insulting to me. I'm done! You go and do what you've planned, and when you find out what a mistake you've made let me know, and we'll have some basis to go on. As things are, I've nothing further to say. Of course, if you change your mind before we leave why you can go along yet, but I suppose that's too much to expect of a little silly head like you. You've made your bed and you'll have to lie on it. No, don't say another word! I'm done!" And he stalked off upstairs without even looking at the nice supper she had prepared at such pains.

That last night in her dear old home was a most unhappy one for Marion. She did not sleep until almost daybreak and then from sheer exhaustion. It was being worse than even her wildest fears, but there was some relief that at last it was out and there was nothing more to dread.

The next morning she came down pale and sorrowful and prepared the last meal in the old home, and then slipped up the back stairs as the others came down the front ones and began to roll up the mattresses and fold sheets and pillow cases, and stuff them into the drawers that had been left unlocked to receive them.

She was everywhere at once it seemed, helping, bringing labels when they were needed, always knowing where the hammer and scissors and cord had been laid down, always knowing just which article of furniture Tom wanted the men to take next to pack in the car.

It was thus she happened to be in the den when the movers came in to take her Father's desk out. It was swathed in burlap, and Marion's eyes filled with wistful tears as the men lifted it up to carry it out of the room. Her father's desk, and she would likely see it no more. Why hadn't she asked Tom to let her have it? Still there would scarcely be room for it in her tiny room. She must let it go. Perhaps, later, when Tom became more reconciled to her new life, he might be willing she should send for it. She could pay the freight on it herself. But now she must let it go.

As the movers passed her she noticed a brown envelope slipping down farther and farther from behind the drawers at the back of the desk, it was more than two-thirds protruding when they reached the door, and impulsively she stepped forward and twitched it out, stuffing it down inside her blouse without looking to see what it was. Probably nothing but an old empty envelope, but it had been her dear father's and it was something she could keep and look at. Anyhow, whatever it was, it would only be lost on the way to the car if it were left sticking out that way. Then, because she was afraid Jennie might notice the stiff bulging and crackling of the envelope, she ran up to her room and slipped it into her little handbag, still without taking time to glance at it.

Tom made one more attempt to reason with Marion, after the last load was gone, and he had time to look around, and see that everything was in order for the new tenants. Jennie and Marion had thoroughly cleaned the house, and there was nothing left to be done but to sweep where the men had brought in dust. So Tom followed Marion into the parlor where she was brushing up nails and papers, and making all clean and neat, and began to reproach her once more. Suddenly she turned on him desperately.

"Tom! Stop! You've always known Father meant me to study. He expected me to stay here in this home that he made for us, and it just breaks my heart to leave it. But since that could not be, I've made no fuss about selling the house because I saw it would break your heart not to have that farm and you had to have the money to buy it. Now, please, please let me stay without being unkind to me. I cannot bear it. But anyway, I've got to stay. I've got to go to lectures and concerts and to night school, perhaps. I've got to have a chance. I would smother if I can't."

Tom, looking into his sister's pleading brown eyes, was startled by her likeness to their father, and he seemed to see something of the spirit of that father, who through all his gentleness had known how to be firm on occasion. So Tom knew it was of no use to say anything more. Marion could not be reasoned out of her "notions."

"It's no use to talk to her, Jen," he said coming back to his wife. "She's set on getting more education, and you can't argue her out of it. Father put it into her head and she's got to try it before she'll be satisfied. It won't take her long to get homesick for us all, and she'll be glad enough to come to us after a few weeks. The best way's to let her see how hard it is to live alone and earn her own living. That's the only way to cure her. She'll soon see her mistake and come running up to the farm."

"Yes, after all the hard work of settling is over," grumbled Jennie, dissatisfied. "You always were too soft-hearted about Marion. I might have known you'd give in. It's lucky the house is sold and the goods gone or she might make you stay here yet."

The next two hours were filled with work and discomfort for Marion; but they were over at last and the girl was glad to bid them all goodby. She was tired of Jennie's alternate sharp words and icy silences; and the parting sarcasms were worst of all. It was only when the babies gave her sweet sticky kisses and Tom gave a burly hug, that a sense of coming loneliness swept over her. But she brushed away the gathering tears and waved a farewell.

Chapter VI

SHE WAS VERY TIRED, more so than she ever remembered
to have been before; but there was a kind of elation upon
her. She still felt the burden of the sorrow through which
she had passed, the strain of the last few days, and the
sudden desolation that had swept over her at parting with
Tom, the only one on earth to whom she could rightfully
say she belonged. Yet she realized that she was standing
upon the threshold of a new life and the whole world lay
at her feet. It was not in any sense self-will that had
brought her to this place. It was an honest desire, a fervid
longing, to get for herself the things her father had striven
to give her and failed. She felt that she owed it to him,
and to the longings that were within her. They seemed
a holy call. Perhaps she was wrong, if she was she wanted
to find it out, but she felt she was right.

If she had stayed in the city for her own pleasure, to
participate in forbidden pleasure, to dress and gad about
and be generally selfish, she told herself this would not
have been the case. But she had not. She had stayed to
make herself the best that herself could be made, for the
glory of God, she added under her breath. Just how her
life could possibly be for the glory of God she did not
understand, only she had been taught early in her youth
that it was, and she had grown up in the firm conviction.
She earnestly desired it to give God as much glory as possible.

So here she was her own mistress. She might apportion
her hours, at least as many of them as she was not using
for the store, in doing what she liked. It seemed wonderful. Some girls would have bought an ice cream cone at
once and then gone straight to the movies, but Marion

entered her freedom with bated breath and wonder in her eyes. Now that she was on her own responsibility she felt she must walk carefully.

She stopped in the station restaurant and indulged in a cup of hot tea and a sandwich, looking about upon her new world with interest.

Over there in the corner were two girls about her own age chummily laughing over the events of the day. Did they care for the great things for which she longed? Or were they trifling life away? From some of their conversation that drifted her way she judged the latter. But anway, whatever they were, she felt a sudden kinship with them and with all the universe of young independent beings like herself. It was a little touch of the modern reaction that had reached her perhaps after all her years of patient sweet subservience, or perhaps it was only her way of choking down the sob that came in her throat when she thought of the dark empty house standing alone, that had been her home for so many precious years, and of the only brother, harsh though he had been, who was speeding toward a new home far away.

She was such a conscientious child that she had to struggle with herself now that the thing was done, not to reproach herself and feel that after all she had been wrong.

It was very dark climbing up her little steep stairway. The landlady held a candle and apologized for a broken gas fixture that made the candle necessary. She said the last lodger had broken it off one night in a drunken rage because he ran into it.

Marion shuddered and escaped into her room which looked weird and desolate with a single gas jet wavering over her paper-wrapped furniture. Her first glance about seemed to warn her that life was not to be all roses yet. She locked her door, remembering with horror a possible drunken neighbor in the room next door. Removing her hat and coat she untied the mattress and pillows and placed them on the bed which she had had the expressman set up when he brought it. She got out some blankets and without further ado dropped herself on the bed under the blankets and was soon asleep.

It was quite late in the morning before she awoke for she had been thoroughly worn out and needed the sleep.

There had been no rousing voice of her sister-in-law to waken her, no sense of duties calling, no clatter of the children.

It was wonderful to just lie still and gradually realize where she was and that no one had a right to call her or demand that she get up till she was ready. This feeling might not last but it was good, for she had been mortally weary, soul and body.

When she finally did get up and went rummaging in her handbag for her watch to see what time it was, she came upon the envelope so hurriedly thrust there the day before and not thought of since. Tenderly she took it out and smoothed its rumpled surface, and was startled to see written on the outside in her father's neat painstaking hand, "MY WILL."

For a moment she sat looking at the words with an almost frightened feeling. There had been a will then, and Tom had not found it! What should she do with it now? Send it to him? Open it? Or would it be better not to even read it, just destroy it now, since all that had been done with the house was now irrevocable. It would only make Tom feel terribly if he had transgressed any of his father's directions, and it was too late to remedy that. Besides, it affected no one but herself probably, for Tom had all there was. Perhaps it might promote more ill feeling between them than there already was. Perhaps she ought to destroy it. Just destroy it without reading it. Perhaps that would be the Christian way.

She held it in her hand, looking at it, half inclined to feel that perhaps it was something she had no right to have.

But then, it wouldn't be right to destroy it either. There might be something in it that they didn't know about, something sweet and precious of which she at least would treasure the thought all her life, and surely she had a right to that since she had relinquished all the rest. It could do no possible harm for her to read it if she kept it to herself. Of course she must not let it influence her in any way, nor let her mind dwell upon anything it might have given her. She had given up her inheritance of her own free will. There was no possible reason why the will should make the slightest difference now.

Slowly, almost reluctantly, she pressed back the unsealed flap of the envelope and took out the single sheet of paper which it contained, and read it through.

The familiar phraseology of the home-made will filled her throat with sobs and her eyes with tears, but she read it through to the end. Her father had left the house and all its furnishings, and his savings fund account, amounting to several thousand dollars, entirely to herself. The life insurance money went to Tom. He called her "my dear daughter," and there was a tender sentence in the will appealing to Tom's chivalry to look out for his sister and see that she was enabled to carry out the plan that he had always had in mind for her education.

She dropped her face on the paper and covered it with kisses and tears. Her precious father! It was like a voice from the other world.

For a long time she sat there on the dishevelled bed, her slender body shaking with sobs, as this tenderness brought back all the years of his constant care.

But gradually she grew calmer, and wiping her eyes sat up and read the paper over again, taking in every detail till it was graven on her mind. She was glad she had read it. Glad her father had been so thoughtful for her. It would make no difference, of course. She had chosen her life. She was carrying out the spirit of her father's wishes, though she did not have his protecting care that he had done his best to make sure for her. But not for worlds would she let her brother know about the will. It could only bring him pain. He had bought his farm, and she knew him well enough to know that while he might not have approved of his father's "notions" as he called them, he was conscientious enough to have carried them out to the letter and said not a demurring word about it. Jennie would have had her say, of course, and a good deal of it, but Tom would have been magnanimous and beautiful about it. He would have probably given up his own desire for a farm, too, and stayed in town to live with her that she might have her home as her father planned.

But perhaps it was just as well that things had turned out as they had. Tom had his wish, and she would be able to carry out hers somehow. God would help her. She felt confident that she could do it. So she would put away the will and keep it among her most treasured possessions, and sometimes when she was lonely and desolate she would take it out and read it just to get the comforting feel of her father's voice to hearten her. But she would leave it where Tom never, never could find it to make him feel uncomfortable.

She bent her head to lay her lips on the signature once more before she slipped the paper back into its envelope, and a whiff of something pleasant and familiar came to her. What was it? Peppermint. How strange. Her father hated peppermint. The odor of it made him really ill. It was likely only the smell of the mucilage on the envelope flap, or perhaps some peculiar kind of paper. Some paper had a strange odor. But it seemed queer that her father's will should smell of it: it seemed somehow a desecration. They never used to eat any candy flavored with peppermint when he was there because he disliked the smell of it so. It was just a little idiosyncrasy of his. Not that he objected to other people eating it, but she had always planned for his comfort not to have the odor of it around when he was in the house. Her mother had been very fond of chocolate peppermints, and so was Jennie. Jennie had made some only a few days before her father died. It hurt her terribly to think that Jennie would deliberately do what she must know would annoy the patient. Jennie had been eating a piece of the candy when she came into their father's room that day after dinner, and Marion had motioned her away quickly. Jennie laughed. She thought it was nonsense. She said people ought not to be humored in such whims, it spoiled them. She had gone away in a huff. There had been smears of chocolate on her fingers and on her dress. Marion remembered how untidy and disagreeable she had looked. Oh, she must stop thinking such things about Jennie! Mr. Stewart had preached about that, some verse from second Peter about "exercising your mind in covetousness." He had said that people exercised their minds in evil thoughts of other people and that was not the way to add to their faith, virtue, and to virtue, knowledge, and all those other things. She must add to her faith, self-control, and keep from thinking unpleasant thoughts about Jennie. She must pray to be kept from having anything in her heart but love for Jennie.

She folded the paper and slipped it into the envelope. Something seemed to catch one corner so that it did not

59

go in smoothly, perhaps it was crumpled from being crushed into her bag. She put her finger inside to smooth it out gently, and came in contact with something rough and hard. She looked and a queer cold feeling came in her throat. It was a tiny piece of chocolate and cream peppermint candy, hardened onto the paper. How did it get into that envelope? Her father's envelope! Her father who hated it and never would have touched any. Jennie! The candy she had made and that she was eating when she left the sick room and went downstairs! Oh, it was unthinkable! But how could she help thinking about it?

There was another thing, how would that will get out of the little strong box where father always kept his papers? He was always so careful. It must have fallen down behind the drawer. Of course, he might have laid it in the drawer sometime, and thought he had put it back in the box. Surely that must have been it. But if it had been locked in the box how could Jennie—how could the peppermint? Oh, she must not think about it! She must not get to feeling that Jennie had done this despicable thing! She would hate her if she kept on this way. And hating, the Bible said, was equal to murder in God's eyes. No, she must not think this of Jennie. But how could she help it? What other explanation could there be? Why had Jennie done it?

A wave of anger swept over her, so that for the instant she was half ready to take the next train up to Vermont and face her sister-in-law with the will and the evidence of her guilt, and demand her rights.

But of course she would not do that. If Jennie had been so untrue Tom must not know it. Tom was honest whatever else he might be lacking in. And if he thought Jennie had done this thing, even with the best of intentions, he would be very severe with her. He might lose all his love for her. And she was the mother of his children. Tom must not know what Jennie had done, if she had done it.

Over and over again she turned the matter, now blaming, now excusing Jennie. Probably Jennie felt that she, Marion, would not suffer. She would have a good home, and all would be well without any financial complications. Mothers looked out for their children in these things, and Jennie was likely to have thought that the will was unfair, that perhaps Marion had influenced her father. Well, perhaps in a way it was not fair to Tom. But her father had always felt that Tom being a man could better look out for himself. Well, whatever it was, of course, she was going to do nothing about it. Of course she was going to have to destroy that will. For now she must not keep it. Tom might find it some day if anything happened to her and it would make trouble all around. Trouble for Tom and trouble for Jennie. No, she must live peaceably. And what was a little money?

And so, before her courage failed her, she laid her lips tenderly once more upon that will, and then resolutely carried it over to the little wood stove that her landlady had had set up in her room, and struck a match from the box on the little shelf by the chimney. She held the will in the stove until it was burned to a crisp. Then she knelt down by her bed and prayed:

"Dear Father, help me to keep from thinking about this. Help me not to blame Jennie unjustly, and to be able to forgive her if she did it, and help me never to mention it or make any trouble about it."

Quite simply she arose and put it away forever from her mind as a question that had been settled once for all, and must not be opened again. It was the kind of thing her father had taught her to do, to be what he called "square" and "Christian." That word Christian in his opinion covered everything that a meek and quiet spirit should have before God, living in this world but not of it. Of course there would be temptations to think hard thoughts of Jennie now and again, but she must resolutely put them from her each time they came and pray for strength. That was the only way to live at peace with all men in this world.

And so, when she was dressed she tried to turn her thoughts to the new life before her and keep them from straying back to that will.

Two whole days she had before her, besides the Sabbath, ere she must begin her work in the store. In that time she could get nicely settled and know just how to arrange her daily plans. She arose with a zest for life that the night before she had not dreamed she could feel.

Her breakfast was a ten-cent box of crackers from the little grocery around the corner and an apple that Nannie had pressed upon her at parting. Nannie more than the other children had cared for her Aunt Marion.

Scrubbing was the order of the morning, but after everything was clean and shining Marion decided to invest a very little of her precious money in brightening up those dingy walls. If she only could find some cheap paper, she could put it on herself. Jennie and she had often done it. Sometimes one could get paper for very little if the pattern was out of fashion. And a very tiny can of paint would freshen up the dirty woodwork. The walls and paint were smoky, and she could not feel comfortable with them that way. With quick resolve she hurried out to the stores, and came back in an hour armed with rolls of paper, a tiny pot of gray paint, a bucket containing ten cents' worth of paste, and a great paste-brush which the paper-hanger had good-naturedly lent her.

That night saw the dingy walls covered with a pretty creamy paper in simple design. It made a wonderful difference in the room, and the wavering gaslight seemed to give forth twice as much light as before. When she had made up her bed and crept sleepily into it she felt that she had accomplished a great deal. To-morrow she would paint the woodwork and arrange the furniture. Then she would be ready to live.

The old landlady looked in toward noon, opening cautiously the door in its fresh coat of paint. Marion was putting down her rugs. On a chair by the window stood a hyacinth in bloom, one that the girl had been nursing all the spring. Its pale pink blossoms gave forth a rich fragrance, not altogether hidden by the clean smell of the paint. Over the footboard of the white bed hung two white muslin curtains ready to be put up when the paint was sufficiently dry. The white bureau was arrayed in its dainty appointments, and the china pitcher and bowl were washed and in their places. Near the other window stood the willow rocker and the little writing-desk close by, with its modest array spread out and a small rack of books atop. The old woman looked and looked again.

"My land!" she exclaimed in an awed voice, "I didn't suppose you could make it look like that! It's worth having you up here just to think there's a place like this in the house. I believe it'll kind of rest me to remember it."

Marion laughed happily, and looked around upon her

abiding-place. It was better than she had dared hope, and she rejoiced in it. There might be trials ahead of her, but there would be this quiet, sweet spot away from everything.

"I just stopped up to say I'd be pleased to have you take Sunday dinner with me to-morrow if you care to. You ain't barely settled yet, and I don't suppose you'll mind not going out this first Sunday. It'll be quite a thing to have a pretty young lady like you at my table."

Marion thanked her, and accepted the invitation, reflecting that she not only had a home, but had already gained a friend in her queer-looking landlady.

The new life was full of novelty, and Marion entered upon her duties in the store with a zest and energy that would have amazed her scornful family, who were hourly expecting her repentant return to their protection. The ribbons were a constant source of delight to her. She loved to handle them, as she loved all beautiful things; and her shy, accommodating ways made her at once a favorite with her customers.

This would have brought her enemies among her co-laborers, had she been less humble or less willing to learn.

When she had her lunch hour, one of the girls in the aisle, perhaps sent by the head of the department, Marion was not sure, smiled at her and asked if she would like to go with her to lunch that day.

She was a girl with closely cropped hair and a flimsy little black satin dress made very short and tight. Marion felt that it was not quite modest, but the girl had a pleasant smile and a hearty voice, and she was really frightened at the idea of making her way alone to the lunch room in the store where most of the girls took their noonday meal.

"You don't know the ropes, do ya?" asked the other girl. "I'll putcha wise. You don't wantta order rice pudding, it's the limit, but the cocoanut pie is a humdinger. You order cocoanut pie. You like cocoanut dontcha?"

"Oh, I like almost anything," laughed Marion to cover her embarrassment. "But don't they have anything but desserts? I've got to be economical till I get started. I'm quite on my own, you see."

"Oh, we're all in that boat, sister. But gimme the pie every time. I havta eat just plain food enough at home. Pie and coffee's what I eat every day. I can't stand soups and slops and I'm sickta death of sanderiges, any kind.

Meat ur cheese, ur some kinda grass, it's all the same to me. They stick in my throat. Gimme me pie an' coffee an' I'm O.K."

"But I should think you'd get sick living on things like that all the time. I haven't been used to it. I'm sure it wouldn't be good for me."

"Sick? Me sick? I should worry. Get off a day then. You're 'lowed a sick day now an' then, you know, an' b'lieve me I get 'em every time. Nothin' coming to me I don't take. It don't pay not to. Ya havta look out for yerself. Nobody else's goin' to look out for ya. Here we are. Now, where you wanta sit? There's a place over there. Some of the crowd from my department there, too. I'll introduce ya. Say, whyn't ya bob yer hair? Make ya a lot more popular. I know they say it ain't being done any more, but look around. I tell ya, look around. Do you see another girl ain't got her hair bobbed? Besides, if the fashion really changes it'll be easy enough to tie some on. Keep yer own an' tie it on with a net over it an' nobody'll ever know. Besides, when that time comes you'll have plenty o' company. Everybody else gotta grow hair, too. Say, yer awful pale. Dontcha wantta borrow some of my lipstick? Ya won't get anywhere with some of the fellas if yer not upta date."

"Thank you," smiled Marion inwardly aghast, "I don't think I'll bother. Tell me, why should I want to get anywhere with the fellows. I don't go out much, and I don't know any of them, you know."

The girl laughed loudly:

"Oh, that's a good one. You gotta good sense of humor, ain't you? Say, I b'lieve I'm gonta like you, but I do wish you'd bob your hair. I'll take you ta my barber ef ya will. They do a dandy cut, makes ya look just like a boy."

"Oh, but I don't think I care to look like a boy," smiled Marion. "I prefer to look like what I am."

"Aw, get out. You look just like a last century school ma'am. You don't wantta, do ya?"

"Well, why not?" asked Marion brightly. "I've been trying for several years to be a school teacher."

"Good-night! You? A school teacher? Whaf-for?"

"Why, I think I'd like it. I love to teach anything."

"Good-night! I don't. I hadta go down and teach a new girl howta tie up packages before I left that department, and I thought I'd pass out. Why she was the dumbest thing you ever saw. She didn't even know how to curl the string around her finger to break it. Actually! Yes, that's right! I certainly was glad when I got her off'n my hands. Whadda ya wantta teach for? We have lots better times here. D'ya play anny instrument? They have an orchestra here, an' ya get time off ta practise, an' there's a lot of dandy men there. There's one fella there, he's married, but he don't care, he carries on just like he was a young fella, an' he brings us chocolates, and we certainly have the time of our life. We write notes, too, an' goodnight! You oughtta see the note I got last night! He's some baby the man that wrote it. He don't care what he says. I said, 'Ya think yer smart, dontcha?' but he knows I won't stand fer everything, that baby does. Say, didn't you meanta order coffee? Just milk? My word, you're a good little girl, ain't ya? But you'll get all over that here. Say, you got pretty eyes. When I first saw ya I says to myself, 'I bleeve I am gonta like that girl. I'll get her fer my buddy.' The girl I been goin' with was jealous of a man I know, an' I'm off her for life. Say, will you wait fer me when we go home? They'll let you off early 'cause it's your first day, an' you wait down by the girl's dressing room, right by the lockers, ya know. I'll be out as soon as I can, but you wait! Oh, yes, my name's Gladys Carr. What's yours? Marion? Say, that sounds real old-fashioned. It sorta fits yer eyes. But I think you oughtta put on some rouge. You're too pale."

She rattled on during the whole noon hour, with just a nod of assent now and then from Marion, and Marion went back to her counter rather shaken in her ideas, but wholly entertained and somewhat refreshed on the whole. After all, wasn't this girl going to be rather good for her in a way? One ought to know all sides of the world to understand what they were thinking about, and now she came to think of it, perhaps she was a bit old-fashioned. Certainly she didn't look much like the rest of the girls in the store, and perhaps that would work against her in the long run. She might lose her position. They might not want a queer-looking girl around.

On their way back to their department, they passed one of the long mirrors with which the store abounded, and Marion studied her own slim little figure in its ill-shaped brown dress that she had worn for best, two years. It never had been a becoming brown, and Marion's artistic soul would not have chosen it, but it was made out of an old dress of her mother's, which she had felt she ought to use up. She had helped a neighboring dressmaker to make it just before her father was taken sick, and it had seemed a very nice dress at the time. It was too long, of course. Strange she hadn't noticed how much longer her dresses were than those other girls were wearing. Of course, some of them wore outrageously short dresses, but one didn't have to go to the extreme in anything, and now she saw herself through Gladys Carr's eyes, she realized that some changes could be made to great improvement and were perhaps due her employer. Not that she meant that Gladys Carr was fitted to be her mentor, but Gladys had spoken frankly from her point of view, and it had really opened her eyes to defects in herself that she ought to remedy.

She watched people all the afternoon, when she was not actually employed, and studied her own raiment with a view to reconstruction. She had not realized how out of date she had allowed herself to get while she was shut up in the house nursing. Perhaps that was the reason those girls in the church had looked at her so contemptuously. Well, that was something that must be remedied. Everyone ought to be as good looking and fittingly clad as was possible under their circumstances, and there were things she certainly could do if she set about it, to remedy her defects, although she had no intention of painting her lips, or wearing earrings, or making her dresses as short as those her new friend wore. Her own fine sense taught her better.

Following the innate guidance of her own artistic soul, the next day, when she had a few minutes off, she found her way to where the imported dresses were on display, and hastily reviewed them. She selected three or four from the motley array that appealed to her as being modest and lovely and fulfilling all the lines of beauty and form and color that should be in a dress and studied them carefully.

That evening she sat up late by the light of her wicked little gas jet sewing a deeper hem into her gown, and laying a couple of pleats that brought it more into fashion's subjection, and the result really did seem to justify her hard work.

It was lucky for her that she had fingers that could fashion almost anything she saw out of whatever material was put before her. Of course, she had little material with which to work, and no money at all to buy any, but she managed to do wonders with her old dresses.

This occupation served two purposes. It gave a new interest to the first few days of loneliness, and it made her look much more like other girls. She resolved that as soon as she could conscientiously afford it she would buy herself one or two of the cheap pretty little dresses that were for sale in the basement. As an employee she could get a discount, so it would not cost so very much, and, of course, she must not look dowdy.

She learned to dress her hair, too, in a more modern way, and it was wonderful how becoming it was.

"Oh, I like your hair, Marion Warren," cried out Gladys Carr, the first morning she appeared with it waved away from her face, piled high in the back, and fastened with an old tortoise-shell hairpin of her mother's. "Oh, isn't that just precious, girls! Look at her! Say, isn't that the cats?"

Marion colored a little at the expression of her friend's interest, but was encouraged and made to feel less shy by the kindly approval of the other girls.

Gladys gave her another hint about lipstick and rouge that day but she shook her head decidedly.

"No, Gladys, I don't like it," she said firmly. "I'll never do it. It doesn't seem nice to me. And, excuse me, but really it doesn't even seem beautiful. It looks so unnatural. It really seems kind of ghastly, just as if a person had died and had been painted up to look like life. I can't bear those dead whites, and vivid reds, nor the Indian colors, either. You never saw a living soul look like that. You can't imitate pink and white health, it has to grow. I'm going to take some exercises at night, perhaps take some walks, and breathing exercises and see if I can't get some real pink in my cheeks, but if I don't I'm not going to paint it on!"

"My soul!" said Gladys Carr looking at her earnestly, "you're awful queer, but yer nice. I 'bleeve I like ya just as ya are! There ain't many I'd say that to, though, I can tell ya."

Then spying another girl passing out the door she lifted up her voice and yelled:

"Say, Totty Frayer, 'was't choo took my pencil off'n my counter this morning when I had my back turned gettin' that spool of silk? I'd liketa know where ya got the nerve! I never done nothing like that ta you. I'd be pleased ta have ya return it. I need that pencil. Get me?"

It was not many days before Marion began to feel more at home in the store, and had other friends besides Gladys Carr. And little by little even the most flapperish flappers among her fellow-workers began to be nice to her. For was she not unfailingly nice to them. She was always ready with a smile to stay after hours in the place of some girls who had a headache, or wanted to go to a moving-picture show that evening, and had to hurry home. She never complained when it was her turn to stay, and she would always cut short her precious lunch-hour five minutes at the request of someone who wanted a bit more time, and asked her to come back early. The ripples in her brown hair and tender lights in her brown eyes were pleasing to look upon and have about.

She was the kind of girl that men admired from a distance, yet not the kind they asked to go with them to the theatre, or presented with flowers and candy; nor did they dare joke with her. They respected her, and let her alone. She made no advances and answered all their conversation shyly, and never thought of lingering about in their way. They thought she was above them, and she was. Nevertheless, she missed much pleasant companionship she might have had, and they missed her guiding presence, which might have been an inspiration to them if they had but understood.

So she passed in and out among them, handling her pretty ribbons, smiling cheerily always to customers and fellow workmen alike, eating her cheap meals gratefully, and hoarding her pennies most carefully.

She drank a good deal of milk; that was cheap, and it gave a pretty roundness to her cheeks and a clearness to her complexion that made her all the more attractive. It had been scarce at home since her father died; there were so many babies to drink milk that there had been very little left for Marion. Besides, Jennie told her she was too old to drink milk; that was children's food and it was extravagant for a grown person to drink it. After that Marion drank no more milk. But now it was the cheapest thing on the menu. A little bottle of rich, creamy milk and a dainty bundle of shredded-wheat biscuit or crackers done up in waxed paper, made a cheap and attractive breakfast or supper.

Then it was a real relief to feel that when her day's work was over her time was really her own. There were no little stockings to mend, nor dishes to wash, nor endless demands upon her precious evenings; and she might read to her heart's delight. Sometimes she felt selfish in her joy over this; yet her conscience told her it was her right to have a little time to herself for improvement, and the books she chose were good and helpful ones, not always just for amusement. Biography, history, and stories were well blended in her self-prescribed course. She joined a summer class in English literature, and took real pleasure in going further in the study that had been interrupted when her school-days suddenly came to an end.

The summer drew on, and the days grew hotter. The little third-story room with its pretty dormer-windows was absolutely breathless. She kept the fact from her inner consciousness as long as possible, and then one stifling night when she slept but little she acknowledged it to herself, and accepted it along with the great loneliness that was gradually growing in her heart, and decided she was glad to be here anyway in spite of heat and solitude.

There were wonderful concerts in the department store, and sometimes the sound of them floated faintly as far as the ribbon-counter. Then it seemed that angels might be lingering above and watching over her work.

But the summer was long and the heat intense. Sometimes even her enthusiasm lagged, and her step grew less elastic. Shredded wheat and cheap dinners palled, and everything in the restaurant smelled alike. Cooking over gas was hot work, and trying to read in the tiny oven that her little top-floor room had become was impossible. She took one or two evening trolley rides to cool off, because the heat at home seemed unbearable; but the getting home alone late frightened her. She was timid about going out at night alone.

She might have had company among her acquaintances in the church, perhaps, but she was so far away now that she seldom went except on Sundays; and, besides, the ones who would have appreciated her fine, sweet friendship did not know her, and knew not what they missed; and the others would have voted her "slow."

It was September when the symphony concerts were brought to her notice by the conversation which she overheard between two customers who had the same seats from year to year and were enthusiastic music lovers. This fired Marion with a desire to get a season ticket and go herself. Why had she not thought of it before?

She inquired about the sale of tickets, and arranged to be among the first in line at the office the morning the sale began. A young man, who stood just behind her in the line, watched her eager face as she asked questions about the seats. Her simple acknowledgment to the apathetic boy behind the ticket-window that this was the first time she had attended the concerts, and that she did not know how to choose her seat interested him. He felt like shaking the youth into a sense of his duty, and was relieved when the girl quietly selected for herself one of the very best seats of those open for sale, an end chair on the middle aisle, about half-way up in the top gallery. As she counted out the dimes and quarters and a worn bill or two, the watcher somehow felt they were won with the girl's life-blood, and her eager, speaking face told how much the tickets meant to her as she folded them into her small, cheap purse and slipped away from the rail. The man who followed her promptly bought a seat for the season one row up and across the aisle from the one she had taken, instead of the balcony seat he had intended to get. He was interested to see the look of this girl when she should hear her first symphony. Would it bear out the impression her face had already given him? It was an idle whim, but because it pleased him he followed it, even though it meant the extra climb to the highest gallery.

It was the night of the second symphony concert when the wonderful thing happened.

Chapter VII

MARION HAD COME EARLY, and was among the first to enter. She loved to watch the vast space blossom into light and life. It was a great world of its own, full of light and sound and beauty. It held her enchanted from the first moment. To-night she had an old pair of opera-glasses that her landlady had hunted out from among her relics of former days. She seemed pleased to let the girl have them, and Marion handled them carefully as if they had been gold set with precious jewels. As a matter of fact, they were covered with worn, faded purple velvet, and looked exceedingly shabby and old-fashioned; but the wonders that they opened up to the girl were just as great as if they had been fine and new.

She climbed the great staircase, and stole down the velvet-covered steps to her seat as if entering a sacred precinct. But she started and looked around when she came to her chair. The seat was turned down as if someone had been sitting there, while all the other seats were still turned up, awaiting their occupants. But the strangest thing of all was that on the seat lay a great, long-stemmed rose, half open. It was one of those rare, dark crimsons whose shadows have hints of black velvet and whose lights glow like hidden fire. From out its heart there stole a fragrance, subtle, heavenly, reminding one of gardens long ago, of rare old lace and lavender and fair fine ladies of an ancient type.

Marion caught her breath in ecstasy, and stooped as if the rose had been a little child, then looked around again to see to whom it might belong. But there was no one about save two elderly women away around the horseshoe circle at the end, and a man on the other side, to whom

71

obviously it could not belong. She had the whole middle section to herself just now, and the lights were not turned up yet to their full power.

Perhaps someone had mistaken his seat, and going away, had forgotten the flower, and might be coming back for it in a moment. Surely no one would forget a bud so exquisite. She lifted it and breathed its fragrance, then looked furtively toward the elderly women. Finally she made her way over to the corner where the two women sat, and asked whether they had lost a flower; but they looked at her coldly and answered, "No," as if they thought her intruding. She went back to her seat, and turning down the next chair laid the rose carefully on it with many a tender look and touch and a wistful breath of its sweetness.

The hall was filling up now, and she found great pleasure in using her opera glasses, watching all the people who came in, noting their beautiful gowns and wraps or trying to think out the stories of them all in their relation one to the other. But all the time there was the breath of the rose and the pleasant consciousness that it was beside her. She never doubted that its owner would return and perhaps through some mistake try to claim her seat as well as the rose. But until he or she came she would enjoy the luxury of the presence of the flower.

She was absorbed in watching the musicians come to their seats with their instruments, when suddenly the owner of the next chair appeared beside her. She stood haughtily in the aisle, a large woman with a wide sweep of cloak trimmed with imitation ermine. Marion, suddenly aware of her presence, dropped her opera glasses into her lap, and shrank into insignificance; but the large lady still waited.

"Please remove your flowers from my chair," she demanded icily; and Marion, feeling that the rose was a friend she must guard till it came to its own, quickly lifted the lovely flower and laid it on her own lap, while the ponderous person settled herself to her own satisfaction, and ignored her.

No one came to claim the rose and Marion felt that the concert had been a double pleasure because of having it. But she waited after others had gone out and looked about in a troubled way. What should she do with it? Surely the owner must have discovered its loss by this time. She went shyly, hesitantly, toward one of the guards in the hall and told him someone had left the flower on her chair. He looked at the stately flower and at the plain young woman who held it, and smiled indulgently.

"I guess it's yours, lady," he said. "Nobody would come back after them kind of things. Whoever dropped it has plenty more where that come from."

"Oh, do you think so?" sighed Marion, and sped away with her treasure out into the darkness.

Up in the little top-floor room the rose glorified everything. She put it in a slim glass vase that had belonged to her father's mother; it was one that Jennie had always called old-fashioned. The dusky velvet warmth of the rose seemed to be at home. The girl hovered about it, taking little whiffs of its intoxicating sweetness; she had laid her cheek softly against its wonderful petals and was happy. She went to sleep making up stories of how it got into her chair, but never by any chance did she happen on the right explanation.

The next day she wore the rose to the store. It must stay with her while it lasted. She could not let it waste its sweetness all alone. That day everyone came to smell her rose and ask her where she got it, and when she said "I found it," they thought she was joking, and rallied her upon her friend, the giver, wondering why she was not willing to confess, and speculating on who it could be.

There are some people whose physical make-up is so constructed that a flower cannot live long near them, but seems to be burned up, smothered, choked, just by lying on their bosoms. But that rose seemed to love to lie near Marion, and to gain extended life from contact with hers. She kept the rose in her wash-bowl under a wet newspaper that night, and the next day it was almost as fresh as ever. Again she wore it, making all the girls marvel and declare it was another flower. The third day she still wore its crimson softness, no longer stiff and fresh, yet beautiful in its fading limpness. The fourth day she gathered its dropped petals wistfully and laid them in a drawer with her handkerchiefs. She would keep their fragrance after their beauty had departed.

The rose was still a pleasant memory on the night of the next symphony concert, and as she came down the velvet stairs to her seat, she was smiling at the thought of it and wondering again how it came there.

73

Then suddenly she paused beside her seat, and drew a quick breath, passing her hand over her eyes. Did she see aright? It was there again! The great dark burning rose. Every curl of the petals seemed the same. Was she dreaming, or was this an hallucination?

As before, there was no one near who seemed to have any connection whatever with the flower, and finally she managed to gather it up softly and sit down in a little limp heap with the flower lying against her breast where her lips could just touch it and its breath steal up into her face. If anyone were watching, he must have thought it a lovely picture. It was as if the first flower had been human and beloved, and had come back to its own from the dust of the grave. This time the girl took the flower to herself, and without trying to fathom its secret, delighted in the thought that it was hers. It seemed to her now that it had a personality of its own and that it had come to her there of its own will.

When the music began, she rested her head against the high back of the seat and closed her eyes. It seemed the voice of the rose speaking to her inmost soul, telling of wonders she had never known, great secrets of the earth; the grave of the seed, and the resurrection of the leaf and flower; the code of the wind's message; the words of a brook; the meaning of the birds' twitter; the beating of the heart of the woods; the whisper of the moss as it creeps; sound of flying clouds on a summer's day. All this and more the rose told her through the music, until her heart was stirred deeply and her face spoke eloquently of how her whole being throbbed in tune to the sound.

The girls in the store exclaimed with laughter and jokes over the second rose; but it seemed too sacred to talk about, and Marion said little, letting them think what they pleased. For herself she tried not to think how the rose came to be in her chair. Since she had looked into the handkerchief-box and found the dead rose-petals still lying sweet and withered, and two days later when she laid the second rose in its lovely death beside the first, she resolutely refused to think how it came to be hers. It was enough that two such flowers had come to her. She did not want to think that perhaps they had been meant for another, and someone was missing what had made her so happy.

The night of the fourth concert her heart beat excitedly. She had told herself a hundred times that of course there would be no rose this time, that whatever happening had given her the two roses could not of course in reason continue; yet she knew that she was expecting another rose, and her limbs trembled so that she could hardly climb the stairs to the gallery.

It was later than she had ever come before. She had felt that she must give some other one a chance to claim the flower if it were really there. There were people sitting all about the middle aisle. The large lady with a fur wrap lying across her lap was there, bulging over into Marion's seat. Marion tried not to look at her own chair until she was close beside it; and she walked down the steps slowly, taking long, deep breaths to calm her tripping heart; but every breath she fancied heavy with rose perfume, and before she had quite reached her place she saw the chair was down, and a great green stem stuck out into the aisle three inches!

There it lay in all its dusky majesty. Her rose! as like the other two as roses could be. It nestled to her heart as if it knew where it belonged, and no one seemed to think it strange that she had taken it as her own.

Marion wore to-night her last winter's black felt hat with a new black grosgrain ribbon put on in tailored fashion by her own skilful fingers. She was learning rapidly how to look like other people—nice people without spending much money for it. The severe little hat was most becoming to her.

More than one music-lover turned to look again at the fresh, sweet face of the girl with the great dark rose against her cheek. Her lips moved softly on the petals as if caressing them, and her eyes glowed dark and beautiful.

That night there grew in her the consciousness that there was intention in this flower, and behind it someone. Who?

The thought made her tremble with fear and delight. Who in all the wide world could care enough for her to put a flower in her chair every night? She was half frightened over it. It seemed not quite proper, yet what was wrong about it? And how could she possibly help it? Throw the flower on the floor? Crush it? Leave it where she found it? Impossible. The flower appealed to every longing of her nature, and she could no more resist the gift of the rose than the rose itself could resist the rays of the sun and turn away to shadow.

Surely the most scrupulous could not find anything wrong in her accepting this anonymous gift of a single wonderful blossom, so long as no further attempt at acquaintance was made. It might be some girl like herself, who liked to do a kind act; or some dear old lady who had seen the loneliness in her face; or some—well, it didn't matter who. There never seemed to be anyone seated around her who was not nice and refined and respectable looking, and utterly beyond any such thing as flirting with a shabby little person like herself. She would just take the flower as a part of her concert, and be happy over it, letting it sing to her again, during the days that it lasted, the melodies that lifted her soul beyond earthly disappointments and trials.

She looked around again as she went slowly out with the others, this time holding her rose boldly close to her face, and taking deep breaths of its sweetness. She wanted to make sure to herself that there was no one about her from whom she would not like to have taken the rose.

As she looked up her eyes met those of a young man just ahead of her in the throng. He was good looking enough to be noticeable even in such a crowd. There was something about him that gave instant impression of refinement and culture. Though his eyes met hers, it was but for an instant, with a pleasant, unintimate glance, as one regards the casual stranger who for the time has been a partner in some pleasure.

Yet somehow in that glance she sensed the fact that he was of another world, a world where roses and music and friendships belonged by right, and where education and culture were a natural part of one's birthright like air and food and sunshine. It was a world where she could only steal in by sufferance for an hour, and that at the price of her little savings and much self-denial. Yet it was a world which she could have enjoyed to the utmost. She sighed softly, and touched her rose gently once more with her lips as if to assure herself that so much of that world was really hers, at least for to-night.

That night she slept with the rose on a chair beside her, and she dreamed that a voice she had never heard before whispered softly to wonderful music, "Dear, I love you." She could not see who spoke, because the air was gloomed with dark rose-leaves falling and shutting out the light; only amid that soft, velvety fall she could hear the echo, "Dear, I love you."

It was very foolish, the whole thing, she told herself the next morning with glowing cheeks. She positively must stop thinking about who put the flowers in her chair, and just enjoy them while they lasted. Very likely there wouldn't be any more, anyway. She must expect that, of course. If anyone was doing it for fun, the freak would not last much longer.

She went humming down the stairs toward her work that day, with the rose on her breast and a happy light in her eyes in spite of all her philosophy. Somehow those roses made her little top floor seem more like home, and drove the loneliness from her heart.

The roses did not stop; they kept coming, one every symphony night. The good looking stranger was usually in his place, but their eyes never met. She glanced back once or twice shyly, just to see who was near her; and always he seemed in his cultured aloofness to be a type of the world of refinement. But he never looked her way. He did not even know she was there, of course. His was another world.

She felt quite safe to glance at him occasionally, as one glances at an ideal. It could do him no harm, and it was good to know there were such men in the world. It made one feel safer and happier about living, just as it was good to know there was a great symphony orchestra to which she might listen occasionally.

One night it rained, but not until after the concert had begun. The sky had been clear at eight o'clock, with the stars shining and no hint of a coming storm. When the concert was out, and the stream of people had reached the great marble entrance where the cream of society lingered in delicate attire, awaiting their automobiles, the rain was pouring down in sheets and the heavens were rent with vivid flashes of lightning and crashing thunder.

Marion in dismay, umbrellaless and rubberless, lingered until all but a few were gone. Then, stepping outside under the metal awning that covered the sidewalk to the curbing, she decided that she must go home. It was getting very late, and there seemed no sign of a let-up.

She did not like to linger longer alone. There were only men left now, and they were glancing at her. She felt uncomfortable. In a moment more the doors of the Academy of Music would close, and she would be left standing in the dark, wet street. She could not walk home, and must sacrifice a few cents of that hoarded sum which was growing toward next winter's symphony concerts, and perhaps a lecture or two in between.

The car came, and she made a dash through the wet, and gained the platform. It was only a step; yet she was very wet, and her heart sank at thought of her garments. She could not afford to replace them if they were spoiled.

The car was full, and she could barely get a seat, squeezed in between two cross fat women. Marion thought with a sinking heart of the half-block she must walk in this driving storm when she reached her own corner. She could not hope to protect herself. She must make up her mind to face it, for the rain was pelting down as hard as ever.

The car stopped at her corner, and she stood for just an instant gasping on the step before she made the plunge into the downpour, expecting to be soaked to the skin at once; but to her surprise she felt only a few sharp spatters in her face now and then and the instant chill of water on her ankles as she hurried down the street.

Suddenly she realized that a shelter was over her. Someone, whom she could not see because of the rain in her eyes when she turned her head, and because of the slant of the blackness before her, was holding an umbrella over her as she flew along. She dared not turn to look, and had no breath to speak and thank him. Indeed, so black was the night—for the electric street-lamps were gone out—that it seemed as if an umbrella had stepped impersonally off the car and was conducting her to her home in the teeth of the storm.

A moment more, and she was safe in the vestibule of her abiding-place; and the dark form who had protected her, umbrella and all, was rushing on through the blackness. Oh, why hadn't she drawn him into the shelter until the rain stopped?

"Come back!" she called, but the wind tossed her words

scornfully into her face. Then "Thank you!" she flung out into the darkness, and was it fancy or only the wind that seemed to voice the word, "Welcome"?

She put the thought away with others to keep, and went slowly, smiling, up the stairs, her cheek against the wet rosebud. Someone had taken the trouble in all this storm to protect her. It mattered not who it was; it might be God; it *was* God, of course. The protector had passed on, but it warmed the girl's lonely heart to know that he had cared, that she was not all alone in the wide universe, with no one who knew or thought of her.

Out of the night and blackness had come a helping hand holding an umbrella, and passed on unknown. Why not a rose the same way? She must get over the idea that someone was picking her out from the world and bestowing flowers upon her. It was utterly absurd and ridiculous, and would put wrong notions into her head, and make her dissatisfied with life.

But the next morning Marion was sick. A cold the day before, and the wetting and excitement had been too much for her. She was not able to go to the store, and had to pay the little colored maid downstairs to send a telephone message for her to the head of her department.

About ten o'clock that morning a boy from the florist's rang the door-bell of the small, unpretentious house where Marion lodged. He carried a large pasteboard box under his arm, and whistled to keep up a brave front. He was to earn half a dollar extra if he performed his errand thoroughly.

He made a low bow to the tattered little maid of all work who held the door half open and giggled at him.

"Hey, kid!" he began in the familiar tone of an old friend; "do me a favor? What's the name of the good-lookin' lady you got livin' here? She's had some flowers sent to her, and I can't for the life of me remember her name. It's got away from me somehow, and I can't get it back. Just mention over the names of the pretty girls you've got boarding here, I might recognize it."

"It ain't Miss M'rion, is it?"

"Miss Marion, Miss Marion what? That sounds as if it might be it. Is she small, and wears a little black hat?"

"Sure!" answered the girl. "That's her. An' anyway she's the only girl here now any more. All the rest is just old women 'ceptin' the 'lect'ic-light men, an' the vaclum-cleaner agent. It couldn't be no other girl, 'cause ther' ain't no other here now."

"What'd you say her last name was? Marion what? I just want to be sure, you know."

"Miss M'rion War'n," replied the girl, and held out her hand eagerly for the box.

"Just give Miss Warren that box, please, and I'll dance at your wedding. So long!" and he dashed away before the girl could get a chance to ask him any questions.

The box contained two dozen great crimson roses, the exact counterpart of those that had been laid in Marion's chair at the concerts.

Chapter VIII

MARION SAT UP IN BED and opened the box in amazement, almost fright. There was no card, nothing even on the box to identify the florist. Just the sweet, mute faces of the lovely flowers.

The astonished, gaping maid stood by in wonder, but could give no explanation save the many-times-reiterated account of her conversation with the boy.

Marion laughed into the box, and cried into it. She had been feeling so lonely, and her head and limbs ached so fearfully, before this box came. Almost she had repented staying in the city. Almost she had decided that probably, after all, her place had been in Vermont, caring for the children and endlessly helping Jennie for the rest of her life. Education and culture were not for her, ever. It was too lonely and too hard work. Too few promotions and too many extra expenses. The loss of this day might cut down her money a little, too, although she was allowed a certain time for sick-leave.

Now, however, things seemed different. The roses had come, and behind the roses must be someone—someone who cared a little. Her cheeks glowed scarlet at the thought. She gave the astonished maid a rose, and sent three more down to her sad old landlady. Then after she had laughed over the roses and cried over them again she put them into the wash-bowl beside her bed, and went to sleep. Someone cared! *Someone cared!* No matter who; someone cared! It was like the refrain of a lullaby. She slept with a smile upon her face; and, while she dreamed, her father came and kissed her, and said as he used to say long ago, "I'm glad for you, little girl, *real glad.*"

When she awoke, the roses were smiling at her, and she

felt better. The next day she was able to go back to the store. She wore a great sheaf of roses this time, and had some to give away, which doubled her own pleasure in them.

It was two days later, while still a dusky red rose was brightening the blouse of Marion's sombre little dress, a young man walked slowly down the aisle in front of the ribbon-counter, and looked earnestly at the array of ribbons as if they possessed a kind of puzzled interest for him. He walked by twice; and the third time, when he turned and came back, two of the girls at the counter whispered about him. They thought he had been sent on an errand for ribbon and didn't know just how to go about it. They had seen his kind before. They presented themselves to his notice with a tempting, "Would you like to be waited upon?" but the young man replied gravely, "Not yet, thank you," and went on with his investigation. He seemed to be interested in the articles in the display-case below the counter, and after watching him amusedly for a minute the two salesgirls retired to a distance to comment upon him.

It happened that during the winter Marion had developed quite a talent for making ribbon flowers and tying bows. During the last three weeks she had been promoted regularly to the little counter where a line of people stood endlessly all day long with anxious, hurried looks, and bolts of ribbon to be tied for "Mary's lingerie," or "a little girl's sash," or "my daughter's graduating-dress," or "a young woman's headdress," or "rosettes for the baby's bonnet."

Marion liked it. Especially she liked the forming of the satin flowers. It was next to working among the flowers themselves to touch the bright petals and form them into shape around the tiny stamens. She was peculiarly successful with ribbon roses, and almost every day had several orders for them for corsage or shoulder.

This afternoon she was sitting as usual before her bit of counter, scissors at her side, spools of wire and bunches of centres close at hand, and a stack of rainbow ribbons in front of her.

The young man gradually progressed down the length of the ribbon-counter till he came to where the bows were being tied; and there he stood a little to one side, watching with absorbed interest as the skilful fingers finished the lovely knots and rosettes and buds.

The counter was busy now, and there was a line of anxious mothers and hurried shoppers waiting to get ribbons made up. The young man watched and waited awhile, and finally, to the immense amusement of the girls at the main counter who had been watching him, he edged up to Marion and spoke to her.

"Are you too busy to select the right ribbon for me and make a rose the color of the one you are wearing? I can wait until you are at liberty if you think you can do it."

Marion looked up. She had not noticed him before, and something in his eyes reminded her of the man at the symphony concerts; but she had never seen that man clearly, save one brief glance. Of course it could not be he. But she answered graciously:

"Certainly, I think I can find that color for you if you can wait till I finish these flowers. A customer is waiting for them."

He bowed and stepped back out of the way, watching the passing throng and waiting until she came to him with the ribbon, matching it to the rose upon her breast. His face lit up with a puzzled kind of relief.

"That looks exactly like it," he said.

"You want a single rose?" she asked, her sweet eyes looking directly at him in that pleasant way she had with all her customers, as if they were her friends. "Is it for the shoulder?"

"Why, yes," said he, a little puzzled. "I don't know how it should be. Make it like some of those in the case. Make it just as you would like to have it." He smiled helplessly, and she answered his appeal with another smile, distant and delicate as a passing bird's might be.

"I understand," she said brightly; "I'll make it pretty"; and she went at the lovely task, deftly measuring and twisting the ribbon into what seemed like a living, breathing rose, and then another tiny bud by its side with a stem and a bit of green leaf. Then she held it out to him. Did that suit him? He said that it did, entirely; and his eyes showed plainly that he spoke the truth.

"How would you—put it on?" he asked hesitatingly,

83

and the girls at the other end of the counter beat a hasty retreat behind the cash-desk to laugh.

"O, what d' ye think o' that?" cried one.

"The dear innocent; is he goin' to wear it himself, or will he stick it on for her?" asked the other, mopping the tears of mirth from her eyes.

But Marion, oblivious, was holding the damask satin rose against her shoulder, and showing how it should be worn.

"Say, it would be the cats to be that man's wife, wouldn't it?" said one of the girls to Marion as her customer received his package and departed with a courteous bow. "Just see the trouble he took to get her something pretty."

Marion's eyes glowed, and all the afternoon she meditated on the careless question. "To be that man's wife," what must it be? How she would like to see the wife who was to wear those roses she had just made! What a dear, beautiful woman she must be! What a charmed life she must live, with someone like that to care for her, anticipate her needs, prepare surprises and pleasures for her! It was something like her own beautiful roses; only of course there could be no one like that behind her roses; only some dear old lady perhaps who had seen her, and maybe loved her a little for the sake of a lost daughter, or friend, or a fancied likeness to someone. Well, it was good that she had her dear roses, and she was glad the beloved wife had someone to care for her. She would like to see her sometime with the roses on her breast. She wondered what she would be like.

And then the day's work was finished, and Marion went home to her fading roses.

There was another church reception early that spring, and a few days before Mrs. Shuttle happened to pass the ribbon-counter and spied Marion:

"Well, I declare. Marion Warren! Is this where you have been hiding all these months. I've wondered why you don't come to prayer meeting any more, and you weren't at the last two church suppers. I thought you promised to help on our committee. Do you know, we have just as hard a time getting someone to wash dishes as ever. Old Mrs. Brown won't come any more, and none of the girls are willing to stick in the kitchen and wear old clothes and keep their hands in dish water. Can't you come down and help us Friday night? We need you badly? There isn't a girl left on the committee has a brain in her head. They're all for beaux and making eyes at the men. I haven't any time for 'em. Do come back Marion just this once and help me. I'm all tired out."

Marion with her usual willingness to oblige finally promised to come. She still felt uncomfortable and humiliated when she remembered that last social she had attended, but what difference did it make? She had grown a little beyond such things she hoped. She had made a new life of her own, and ought to be big enough not to be troubled by being ignored by a girl she used to know just because she was not as well dressed as the rest of them. Well, they could find no fault with her now. Thanks to the store she now knew what one ought to wear and exactly how to accomplish it on a very small income. She had learned that the most expensive models almost invariably chose lines of simplicity, both in cut and decoration, and therefore she had been enabled to select from among the cheaper garments, those which followed this simplicity of good taste. Here in the store, also, she was able to purchase really fine material at very low cost, by reason of the many opportunities to buy remnants, and also by reason of her employee's discount. Therefore Marion no longer felt embarrassed by her awkward garments.

But even though she knew she had a pretty and suitable dress to wear, she did not relish going back among a set of girls who had tried to snub her. It roused feelings which she felt were un-Christian, and unworthy of herself. Nevertheless she had promised, and for this once she meant to go. It would be nice at least to meet the minister's wife again and have a little talk with her. Perhaps she would come down to see her sometime, too. That would be delightful. She might even get an afternoon off and ask her to take a cup of tea with her in her tiny third-story room. Of course, it was not palatial, but it was neat and cosy, and she was sure Mrs. Stewart would not mind having to climb two pairs of stairs just for once. She would not want to ask everybody to come up there, but it would be dear to have Mrs. Stewart. It would be like having a visit from a mother. Perhaps she would even dare to ask her about some of the problems which had been perplexing her.

So Marion agreed to go, and to wash dishes.

When the evening came Marion dressed with special care in a little satin dress of dark garnet which she had bought because it reminded her of the depths of shadow in her roses. It was wonderfully becoming and set off her dark eyes and hair and delicate features perfectly. The sleeves were georgette and showed the roundness of her arms prettily. She took care to arrange the wrists with extra snap catches so that she might unfasten them and roll the sleeves above her elbows when she washed dishes. Also she had provided a pretty white rubber apron with little rubber frills around the edges which covered her satin gown amply, and was becoming enough in itself so that she would not feel out of place among the well-dressed women.

As she got out of the trolley in front of the church and walked down the pavement to the side entrance which was brightly lighted a sudden feeling of the old panic came upon her. She seemed to feel herself about to become the scorn of all eyes, and in spite of all her resolves a longing to flee took possession of her. She looked down at her pretty new patent leather slippers with their modest steel buckles, and her slim gray silk ankles, and remembered that there was nothing noticeable about her garments. She was as well dressed as anyone. There was no reason why she should be singled out for scorn on that score. She looked up to the deep dark blue of the sky above her, set with sparkling stars, and breathed a little prayer: "Dear Father, I'm your child. Help me that I shall behave in a way to bring glory to your kingdom and not discredit. Help me not to be frightened, or be a fool."

Then she stepped into the brightly-lighted vestibule and looked about her.

Mrs. Shuttle was there, looking anxiously for someone. She grabbed her at once eagerly:

"Oh, you've come. I was afraid you wouldn't. My! I'm so glad! My daughter has the grippe and couldn't come at all, and I'm all beat out waiting on her all day. Say, you'll take charge of the aides when they come in and tell them where to put their wraps, and what to do first, won't you? I've simply got to run home and give

Mary her medicine. I forgot to put it where she could reach it, and she's got an awful high fever, and I don't like to leave her without it. And say, after things are pretty well served would you mind staying just to-night and seeing that all the dishes are washed and put away right. You know we've got a new janitor and he doesn't know a thing about where things belong."

Marion promised, though with sinking heart. She had been hoping to get away early and do a little studying before she went to bed. She had joined a literature class, and a class in current events early in the winter, and they were to have examinations soon. She did want at least an hour before she slept in which to study. But it could not be helped of course. She couldn't say no to Mrs. Shuttle when her daughter was so sick. So Marion went into the big bright room resolved to take off her coat and hat and then go at once to the kitchen and stay there. At least she would have plenty to do to fill the evening, and need not bother about having to sit around alone with no one speaking to her. Likely she wouldn't even get a chance to see the minister's wife and give her invitation.

As she came out of the ladies' parlor, where she left her wraps, and started across the main Sunday School room to the kitchen two men stood talking together over by the platform. One of them was the bank president, Mr. Radnor. The other was a stranger whom she did not even notice. She was thinking that she ought to go over and speak to Mr. Radnor and tell him how grateful she was for _his_ influence which had given her such a fine position. Could she do it now while there were only a few people in the room? Or must she wait until he was done speaking to the stranger?

While she hesitated the eyes of the two were upon her.

"Who is that girl, Radnor," the stranger was saying with almost a note of eagerness in his voice.

"Where? Over there by the door? Why, who is she? Let me see. Can that be——? Why, yes, I guess it is that little Warren girl, Marion Warren. Nice little thing. Good girl. She came to me for a recommendation to get a job last spring. I guess she's made good. She's been a member of this Sunday School ever since she was a little tot in the primary. We have a lot of that sort here, you know, good, plain respectable people, never very well off, but

87

make a good living and are good sturdy stock. Makes a pretty good foundation for a church, you know. And you'd be surprised how that class of people give. Better in proportion sometimes than the really well-to-do."

"I'd like to meet her," said the younger man.

"Why, yes, certainly," said the kindly superintendent, a bit perturbed, "but, you know, Lyman, she really isn't in your class. Do you think it wise? It might put notions in her head and she's a nice little thing. Her father was a good man, a sort of saint in his way, you know."

"She looks it," said the younger man earnestly. "And you're mistaken, Radnor, she is in my class. We've been attending the symphony concerts all winter, not exactly together, but her seat was just across the aisle from mine and I've been noticing how she enjoyed the music. So you see we have a common interest. I'd really like to meet her if you don't mind. I'll try not to put any wrong notions in her head," and he laughed amusedly.

"Why, of course, if you wish it. She is a nice child as I told you. I didn't know she cared especially for music. Somebody, probably, gave her the tickets. She couldn't afford to get them herself I'm quite sure, and I can scarcely think she'd have the inclination of herself. But we can manage the introduction casually, of course. You can see what she is for yourself. I don't imagine she's had more than a common school education. The father was a hard worker, and they lived in one of the smaller streets. But see, she is coming this way. It will be quite all right I am sure."

Marion had decided to get her duty over quickly before the arrival of those obnoxious girls, and was walking straight across the room to Mr. Radnor, stranger or no stranger. She wouldn't interrupt them but a second, and she might not get another chance after she went to the kitchen.

She did not have to interrupt them by saying excuse me, as she had planned to do, for she found the two men waiting for her as if they had expected her, and the bank president with his most presidential air greeted her with his smile.

"Why, good evening, Miss Marion, I've been wondering how you are getting on? This is Mr. Lyman. You have met him before, haven't you? And how did you make out at the store? Did you get what you wanted?"

He scarcely gave Marion and the young man an opportunity to acknowledge the offhand introduction before he plied her with his question. But he found to his relief that Marion was not especially interested in the young stranger. She acknowledged the introduction with a smile, and a slight inclination of her head, and turned her eyes at once back to Mr. Radnor's face saying in a business-like tone:

"Yes, Mr. Radnor. I came over here to thank you. I have wanted to tell you before how well I am doing and how much I owe to your kind introduction, but I hesitated to take your time at the bank, and you are always so surrounded after Sunday School that I haven't been able to speak to you."

"You're quite welcome I'm sure," he said genially, almost pompously, young Lyman thought. "I'm very glad it all came out right. Call upon me again any time I can help in any way. I'm always glad to help any of our school, you know. That's what the church is for. Ah, Lyman, Stewart has come at last. Shall we go over and talk that matter over with him? Good-evening Miss Warren. We'll see you again I'm sure before the evening is over. This is a pleasant occasion, isn't it? So nice to get all classes together on a common footing."

They moved away and Marion had somehow the same feeling she had known at the last church social, a feeling of having been put in her place, this time nicely and sweetly, with a smile and an offer of friendliness, but still put in her place.

She did not notice at the moment that the young man had said as he moved away, with a pleasant friendly smile:

"Well, we shall see you again this evening, Miss Warren." It would have made little impression anyway. Of course, he was just being polite, a nice pleasant stranger. Why was there something about his eyes that looked familiar? Mr. Radnor had spoken as if perhaps they had known each other before. He must be some member of the church who had moved away and was back for the evening. Of course, she had never seen him before, yet his eyes had looked familiar. He probably resembled someone she knew in the store. Humanity seemed to be cut off in strips, and some belonged to one strip and some to another. This young man belonged to a pleasant type that had the faculty of making one feel at ease. But what difference? She would probably never see him again, anyway. She would go at once to the kitchen, and would not come out again that night if she could help it. It was probably her own fault somehow that people treated her so condescendingly. But it didn't matter. She was getting too sensitive. She must not care whether people liked her or not. Her lot in life was a lonely one and she must get used to it.

So she made her way at once to the kitchen without further hindrance, and Mr. Radnor, having piloted his man to the minister and talked a few minutes wandered off to talk to another business man who had just arrived, congratulating himself upon the tactful way in which he had managed that introduction. It certainly would have been unfortunate for Lyman to show any attention to that little mouse of a Warren girl. He was fully aware that his own niece Isabel was openly out for that young man's attentions, and he would not like to incur her enmity by having been the one to bring about even a casual friendship between Lyman and a little salesgirl from his Sunday School. If Isabel married Lyman she would be well off in his hands and have made a most fitting match for herself, pleasing to the entire family connection, as well as himself. Lyman was certainly a most unusual young man, wealthy as anyone need ever care to be, and upright in every way. Interested in the church, too, which was most commendable in this modern age of indifference, especially among the young. He certainly was an unusual young man!

Marion reached the kitchen and found three or four women ahead of her, bustling around arranging salad on plates, cutting cakes, making coffee.

They greeted her with relief:

"Oh, here's Marion Warren! Now we'll be all right. She'll do it. Say, Marion, will you go out there and hunt up Mrs. McGovern and ask her which of these cakes she wants cut first? She told me but I've forgotten. It's either the chocolate or the cocoanut, and I don't know which. She'll be mad as a hornet if I make a mistake. And while you're about it, won't you see if you can find Isabel

Cresson anywhere? We haven't enough waitresses and I promised to ask her, but I've got this apron on and my sleeves rolled up and I hate to go out now."

Marion with heightened color, turned to do their bidding, wishing almost that she had not come, if she had to carry a message to Isabel Cresson. However, that of course was beneath her. She must conquer such feelings. She hastened out hoping that the Cresson girl had not yet arrived and she might be able to put the errand off on somebody else. She found Mrs. McGovern easily enough, discovered that the chocolate cake was to be cut first, and after a swift glance around decided to her relief that Isabel Cresson had not yet arrived. She was just skirting the groups that were standing about talking when a lot of girls burst noisily into the room from the dressing room and Isabel was foremost among them.

"Oh," said Marion, "Isabel, I've a message for you."

Isabel turned and stared at her coldly.

"Aw! It's Marion War'n, again, isn't it? I hardly knew ya!"

Marion's cheeks were pink with the slighting tone, but she went on briefly:

"Mrs. Forbes wants to know if you will help out as an aide. She says they haven't enough aides."

"What! Me? Naw indeedy! I nevah tie myself up like that, not this baby. I came to have a good time. Besides I've got a new imported frock on. I'd be sure to ruin it. Just run back to Mrs. Forbes and ask her, what does she think I am? Ask her that for me!" And Isabel's laugh rang out in scorn, which somehow seemed to be turned against Marion, and all the other girls joined in the laugh, and looked at Marion as if she were a doormat. At least that was the way it seemed to Marion.

The color came in a tide into her cheeks now. For a minute she wanted to stand still there and turn on those girls and tell them just what she thought of them. Tell them how rude they were.

Well, what good would that do? And those ugly feelings that came into her heart. They were altogether unworthy of a child of the King. She was routed again. She must not let these girls have such power over her that they could trouble her soul even to having sinful thoughts, for some-

.ow before she realized it, she was saying to herself how she hated Isabel Cresson.

Then instantly came the thought that she had a refuge from all such things. One who was a very present help in time of trouble and she could cry to Him even in this crowded noisy social room. So she lifted her heart for help, and with her head raised in a sweet dignity she began making her way between the people who were coming in very fast now and filling the room. Then suddenly the minister's wife slipped her arm about her and greeted her with a smile as if she were really glad to see her and she felt a sudden rush of comfort. What a silly she was! Was she going to cry right there before all those people? Oh, Jennie and Tom had been right. She was not fitted to go among people. She belonged out on a farm somewhere, where she wouldn't come in contact with the world at all! She must get over such foolishness and learn not to care what those rude girls did. Just because she used to know them at school and had expected them to be friendly. She must not let such things upset her so.

The minister's wife was talking to her, saying dear things about her father, telling her how badly she had felt when her own father had been taken away. Her sympathetic tone seemed healing in its touch. The tight lines around Marion's lips relaxed and she began to look almost happy.

And suddenly the minister loomed in her way in a group of other men:

"Why, here is Miss Warren!" he said heartily. "Glad to see you. You're getting to be quite a stranger here, do you know it? Though you're pretty faithful on Sundays, yet, aren't you? I always see you and try to get down to speak to you, but you slip away too quickly for me. By the way, Marion, you know this man, don't you? Jefferson, you know Miss Warren, surely."

Marion looked up to meet the eyes of the same young man to whom Mr. Radnor had so casually introduced her a few minutes before, and she could not help seeing that his eyes were full of interest. Where had she seen those eyes before? Surely she must have seen him somewhere.

She looked up with a natural little smile to acknowledge the introduction, wondering what to say, suddenly embarrassed by the unexpected sight of Isabel Cresson and

92

her gang bearing down upon them between two groups of people.

Panic took hold upon her again. No, she would not meet those girls now, they would be sure to humiliate her before this pleasant stranger!

The minister was talking in answer to something Lyman had said:

"Yes, I suppose you must have been away at that time. I hadn't realized how long it had been. And you were but a boy when you left. Of course, you wouldn't know the older members of the church well. But your father did. And this young woman's father was one of the salt of the earth, one of our saints, you know. He has just recently been called home."

Marion's heart warmed and went on beating with something like its normal rhythm, and her eyes lost something of their panicky look. Somehow her glance was drawn involuntarily to the eyes of the stranger and she saw that his face was full of sympathy. She gave him a trembling little smile of thanks. That was a beautiful thing for a young man to do, to seem to care about a stranger who was dead, a man whom he had never seen.

She would probably never see this young man again, he was likely a visitor in the town, but she would always remember his look that was a tribute to her father's name.

But there was no time to summon words to answer. Those girls were close at hand, and she could see by the look in Isabel's eyes that she was bearing down upon the young stranger, as one hails an old friend.

She lifted her firm little chin and tried to smile and said hurriedly:

"Please excuse me now, I've promised to help in the kitchen and I think they must be waiting for me!" And she was gone, slipping between the people, and gliding down the kitchen passageway out of sight.

Chapter IX

TO THE YOUNG MAN who watched her hasty retreat she seemed a lovely thing. He noted the delicate profile of her face, the profile with which he had grown familiar in the Academy of Music, watching it to the accompaniment of the world's great music exquisitely rendered. Somehow she seemed to him to be naturally associated with all things fine and exquisite and lovely.

He noticed, too, with kindling eye, the color of her plain little gown, deep crimson, like the shadows in old-fashioned damask roses, and how it brought out the shell pink tinting of her cheeks, and the clear straight pencilling of lovely brow. To the young man the shy lifting of her serious eyes had satisfied all his expectations. If what Radnor had said about her coming from a common family had been true, where and how had such a lovely unspoiled spirit come up through the soil and rudeness of this present world? She was so very different from the girls he saw about him.

He turned about and faced Isabel Cresson, in blue and silver, with her long earrings and her ropes of pearl, her gold boy bob, and her carmine lips and rouged cheeks. Isabel was vivacious and sparkling, gay and full of banter, bold and wise and able to take care of herself, like the present day and generation. But oh, what a contrast! The young man's eyes followed wistfully the girl in the garnet satin, and wished she would come back and talk to him.

"Hello, Jeff!" greeted Isabel. "Never see you any more unless I come to church. You must have got converted over in Europe, you only seem to be on exhibition at a church social. Why don't you come out to the country club and have a try at things. Got the darlingest floor now, the best dancing anywhere around, and the greatest orchestra! It's precious! You haven't heard it yet, have you? And you've been home almost a year! What did they do to you over there? Make an old man out of you? Have you forgotten your old friends? What's that? You're too busy? Oh, Bologny! So's your old man! Come on out on the links Sunday morning and let's play a few holes. Lately I've been shooting down the eighties! Not so bad, what? Come and try me, Jeffy! I'd like a chance to even up some of the old scores when you laid me out at tennis. Swing a racket anymore? We just got four more new courts. The turf is peachy. I can play a precious game at that, too. You ought to try me now! And I've just got the darlingest new racket. I'm dying to try it on somebody. What do you say? Is it a go Sunday morning? What? You got to go to church? Applesauce! Cut it out for once! Well then, make it six in the morning and we'll have coffee at the Club House and get back in plenty of time. Church isn't till eleven. Or I'll get up at five if you like that better. What? Why Jeff Lyman! You're not such an old granny yet that you won't take refined exercise on Sunday? I'd like to know why? I thought you were progressive. Why, I thought you'd been abroad and got rid of all your narrow notions. They're just traditions, anyway, handed down from your family. You know you don't really think there can be anything wrong in going out into the lovely air, walking around after a ball a little while. Why nobody stops at anything like that anymore, at least not any of our old crowd. Why, the minister where friends of mine go even has church real early in the morning so his members can go and then have all the rest of the day for recreation. He says he thinks that's what the Bible means. The Sabbath was made for man. You don't really mean Jeff that you object yourself? Well, of course, in that case we might play Saturday. I have an engagement, but I'll break it for you. Will you do that much for me?"

"I'm afraid not, Isabel," said the young man amusedly, "I've something quite different in mind for that day, too, if it materializes. By the way, didn't I hear somebody say you were going to sing to-night? That will be interesting. You used to have a fine voice when you were a kid. I suppose you've been studying hard?"

Isabel made a wry face:

"Who? Me? Did you ever know me to work hard at anything? Oh, I've been taking lessons, of course. Had a few from that stunning tenor. He's an Italian and he has the most gorgeous eyes. All the girls have a crush on him. But he's married unfortunately and his wife won't give him a divorce. Isn't that tragic? If I was married to a man that wanted his freedom I'm sure I wouldn't object. It seems common to hang onto a person when they want to be free. Don't you think so? I think Europeans are so much more sophisticated in those things. Say, I'm wild to hear all about your experience in Siberia? Wasn't it terrifying? But you were always so brave! Jeff, it's just great to have you home again, and you really must come to the dance next Saturday night. It's going to be simply darling. The decorations alone are costing——"

But Jefferson Lyman's eyes were off at the other side of the room, where a girl in a satin frock the color of old-fashioned damask roses was arranging a table with cups and saucers and sugar bowls and cream pitchers.

"Excuse me, a minute, Isabel," said the young man suddenly, "I want to speak to someone." And he disappeared among the crowd.

A sudden blank look overspread Isabel's face as she watched him go.

"Oh, for cat's sake!" she exclaimed to Aline Baines who acted the part of shadow to Isabel. "How do you suppose he got to know her? Probably that fool Stewart introduced them. He hasn't any more idea of the fitness of things! For a minister he's the limit! I do wish we could go to another church! Now isn't that just enough to make you pass out? And the poor dear doesn't know the difference, of course! Men never do. Fancy! Marion Warren! Aline, we've simply got to rescue the poor man from her clutches. But fancy Marion Warren aspiring to Jeff Lyman! I ask you, did you ever hear the like? I didn't think she had the nerve. But I saw her rolling those big old eyes of hers at him as we came up. Isn't it vexatious? And he hadn't told me yet when he was ready to play golf with me. Come, darling, we've got to go to the rescue."

Isabel and her followers filed hastily through the crowd toward the table where Marion was arranging cups for the expeditious pouring of coffee when the time came to serve everyone at once. Lyman saw them coming, too, and he walked boldly up to Marion and spoke:

"Aren't you going to be free after a while? I'd like to talk with you. I know you've been enjoying the concerts this winter, and I'm longing for a kindred spirit to talk them over with me."

Marion looked up with a sudden light in her eyes. Could she believe her ears aright? Of course, he didn't know what a very humble person she was or he wouldn't likely have spoken to her, selecting her from the whole roomful of girls, but it was so good to have someone speak to her like that, as if she were an equal, as if her opinion on anything so great as music was of any worth!

"Why——" she hesitated shyly with a smile that lit her face into new beauty and fired the soul of Isabel Cresson, coming on in the distance, into new fury, "Why —I—really—I don't know! But I'd love to," she finished impulsively. "I'll try. I've never had anyone to talk over the concerts with. It would be so nice."

"Jeff! You didn't say when you'd be ready to play golf!" broke in Isabel peremptorily. "I'm not going to let you get away without setting a definite date! Oh, is that you, Marion? I just met Mrs. Shuttle and she wants you to go to the kitchen at once!"

The tone was most disdainful, as if Isabel were commanding a poor minion, but for some reason Marion was not frightened. The look in the eyes of the pleasant stranger who had just said he wanted to talk with her about the symphony concerts gave her strength, and she had a quick flash of revelation that God was answering her prayer and standing by her. She flashed a funny little smile at Isabel and answered:

"Oh, you're mistaken, Isabel. Mrs. Shuttle has gone home to take care of her sick daughter, and I'm taking her place for a while. Perhaps you will go into the kitchen yourself and tell the girls I'm ready for them to bring the coffee urn now if they have it filled."

The young man's eyes were dancing with fun, but he stood quietly by watching this little tilt and thinking what a dead contrast these two girls were.

"Oh, really?" said Isabel scornfully. "No, I can't be bothered. What do you think I am? A servant?" and she turned her back on Marion and tried to press her challenge for a game on Lyman.

Marion went on coolly placing coffee cups and giving low-toned orders to the aides who came back and forth bearing dishes, but she was wondering if she had been un-Christian in her reply to Isabel. More than anything else she desired that her life should show forth the glory of God. She had a quiet feeling that God had stood by her, and she must not do the least little thing by word or deed, or even thought that would not be according to His purpose for her life. Her life was meant to show forth His glory, not her own, and perhaps her tongue had got away with her. It would have done no harm for Isabel to think that she had scored a triumph.

Then she heard Lyman's good-natured answer to Isabel:

"Thanks, awfully, Isabel, but I'm afraid I'm not in the market for a game just now. The fact is my time is pretty well taken up——" Lyman was leading Isabel away from the table now, and Marion smiled quietly to herself. Somehow she felt as if she had a champion, someone to take her part against the world. It was a new feeling, for since her father had been taken away she had felt she would never have anyone to care much again. Of course, Tom cared in a way. But Tom was angry with her. In all the winter she had had only one or two brief curt letters from him, and Jennie had written not at all, though she had written to them regularly once a week for a long time until she saw she got no reply. Even then she had tried to keep up a form of correspondence. It might be one-sided, but they should not have it to say that she had not kept in touch with them. And she had sent many pretty little presents, useful things, and playthings, to the children— out of her small salary, too. But still, she had a feeling that she was alone in the world, and if anything hard happened to her, there was not anybody who would care very much. Therefore it was wonderful to have someone be as kind and courteous as this stranger had been.

Presently Lyman disappeared from the group of girls, and she thought perhaps he had gone home. She spied him later when she slipped into the classroom where all the younger boys had congregated to see if they had all been served, and found him with a group about him while he told them stories of his travels.

There was an extra plate of ice cream left on the tray she carried, and Lyman made room for her beside himself and begged her to sit down for just a few minutes and eat it with them. There really was not any good reason why she should refuse. The rush at the coffee table was over and the aides were serving themselves. There was no immediate hurry about beginning on the dishes, and Mrs. Shuttle had returned and would take command for the time, so she sat down, glad that she was in an inconspicuous classroom, rather than out where everybody else was. She did not care to be in the public eye, not while Isabel was about.

It was thus she came to hear some of his wonderful stories, and to listen while he described marvelous pictures he had seen in some of the world's most famous galleries. It was noteworthy that he described those pictures in such a way that even the youngest boy in the group did not grow restless nor lose interest, but kept an admiring eye upon his face and hung upon his every word.

He was describing a picture he had seen in a great art gallery abroad when there came a general stir in the room outside, and the distant clatter of dishes reminded Marion of her duty.

"They are bringing the dishes back!" she exclaimed contritely. "I must go at once. What will they think of me? I promised, you know, but oh, I thank you so much for this! It has been beautiful."

She gathered up the dishes on the tray, and he rose to let her pass, but detained her just an instant.

"Have you someone you must go home with, or may I wait and go with you?" he asked in a low tone.

The soft flush of her cheeks mounted to her forehead, and her eyes were filled with half-frightened pleasure.

"Oh, no! There is no one any more," and her voice had a faint quiver as she spoke; "but indeed you must not wait for me. I shall be very late, and it isn't at all necessary. I am quite used to going alone now. But I thank you very much just the same." She hurried away to the kitchen with a smile, her heart beating high at the thought of what it would have meant to her to have a man like that escort her home. It helped to keep her smile sweet and her eyes unhurt through all the clatter of the kitchen and the reproachful voices that met her and demanded to know where she had been.

The young man lingered idly, watching her for a moment as she slipped away, pondering on the wistfulness of her eyes as she declined his offer. There was a look of resolution in his own eyes.

"I shall wait all right!" he murmured to the red and black figures of the church carpet at his feet.

Marion in the kitchen tying on her little frilled rubber apron was reflecting that the evening had been a rare treat after all its bad beginning, one which she would treasure among her happiest memories. This was the kind of talk for which her beauty-loving soul had longed. Now, she would go the very next night to the Public Library and find some books about those galleries and read and read and read until she knew all that could be known about those pictures and could talk about them intelligently. She wished she might have written down some of the names of the galleries, and the artists he had mentioned. If she ever had opportunity to meet him again she would try to summon courage to ask him to write them down for her. He would think her an awful ignoramus, of course, but it would be wonderful to know.

At last the company in the chapel broke up and the big room was cleared as if by magic.

Lyman walked in a leisurely way around the room examining the inscriptions on the brass plates underneath some memorial pictures that hung upon the walls. He could hear the gentle clink of china and silver in the kitchen. Only a group of Ladies Aiders were left in the big room holding a discussion in the middle of the room about their next bazaar.

The janitor was picking up the lost handkerchiefs and gloves that always accumulate after an affair like this, and the voices of the younger people were heard in the hall saying gay good-nights.

A burst of hilarious laughter came through the swinging door as someone went out, and then a group of pretty girls in bright evening cloaks looked in, jostling one another in the doorway.

"Oh, here he is!" called one, and they all bore down upon him.

"Come on, Jeff!" called Isabel Cresson. "You didn't

come in your car, did you? Uncle Rad says it isn't parked outside anywhere. He wants you to come with us. We'll drop you at your place."

"Thank you," said Lyman politely, "but you see I'm waiting for a friend."

"Oh!" said Isabel, slightly baffled for a moment, "well, bring him along. There's plenty of room. Uncle Rad has the big car."

"Impossible," said Lyman, smiling. "My friend may not be ready to go for sometime, and besides, I have my car. It is parked around the corner tonight. The street was full when I came. Thank you just the same."

Isabel retired somewhat crestfallen, with many a lingering glance backward to discover if possible who was the favored friend.

But at last even the Ladies Aiders departed and Lyman approached the kitchen cautiously.

Marion thought she was all alone in the building with only the janitor out arranging the chairs in orderly rows for Sunday School. When she heard Lyman's voice she started:

"I've come to wipe dishes for you!" he said gaily. "Give me a towel. I know how. I used to do it when I was a little boy."

Marion's heart leaped and then her pleasure was shown in her eyes. He had stayed. Everybody else was gone and he had stayed to talk to her! Of course, he did not realize what an insignificant little girl she was, but that didn't matter for just once. She did so want to ask him some questions about those wonderful pictures and where she could find out more about them. And he was kind. He wouldn't mind if he did find out that she was only an ignorant girl who worked in a store. He seemed to like to help people.

She protested against his working, but he took the towel and went at it as if he really knew how, polishing glasses like an old hand in the kitchen. Marion tied a clean apron around his neck, one that Mrs. Shuttle had left lying on the table, and they worked away as blithely as if they had known each other all their lives.

Of course, it was like Isabel Cresson to make out she had left her gloves or her handkerchief or something and come back for them, just to find out if she could who that

101

mysterious friend of Lyman's was, just to get another word with Lyman himself, perhaps.

She pushed open the silent swinging door and looked in just as Marion was tying the apron around Lyman's neck, and she heard their laughter ringing out in unison, and saw that they were having a genuinely good time together. But they did not see her, and she let the door swing quickly back into place and searched no further for the gloves that were not lost, but went back angrily to the waiting car. So that was what Marion Warren was up to, chasing Jeff! Well, that had got to be looked into. That was not to be borne. Somebody had to warn Jeff. And somebody had to squelch that little upstart of a Marion. The idea! Marion Warren! What could he possibly see in her?

"He's wiping dishes for that egg of a Marion Warren," she announced as she got into the car. "I think you've got to get busy about that, Uncle Rad. I didn't know she was such a sly little cat! Of all the nerve! She was perfectly insulting to me tonight. Answered me back when I brought her a message and tried to make me out in a lie right before Jeff. Was it you who introduced her to him, Uncle Rad? I should think you'd better watch out what you do. Of course, he doesn't know anything about her. He doesn't know what common people they are though I should think he might see if he has any discernment. She doesn't belong in our set at all."

"Well, you see he asked to be introduced," said the uncle apologetically. "It's queer how men will be taken with a pretty face sometimes, and I told him about her, I informed him that she came from plain respectable people, and I really warned him. I shouldn't like her to get any false notions about him. She's a nice little thing and I had a great respect for her father."

"Oh, you needn't worry about her!" said Isabel caustically. "If you had seen her vamp him to-night you'd know she could take care of herself. She's the slyest thing. She kept following him around. Everywhere he turned there she was. Pretty? I don't see how you can say she is pretty! She looks as if she came out of the ark. She looks as if she was so innocent she belonged back in the dark ages. Look at her sallow cheeks and her white lips. She doesn't even know how to make herself look stylish.

She just depends upon old stuff, rolling those great brown eyes of hers and looking demure. Old stuff, all of it. I don't see what makes Jeff fall for it, but he's so fearfully afraid of hurting people's feelings, of course, he'll stand anything. I really think it's up to you Uncle Rad to warn Jeff. He'll get her talked about you see. And I'll make it my business to see that Marion cuts out that kind of thing from now on, or I'll make it too hot for her in this church. I won't stand for it, having Jeff made a goat of."

"There, there! Isabel. Don't get excited," said her pacific uncle. "I'll manage it that Lyman will understand. You keep out of this. It'll all blow over. Lyman doesn't want to get mixed up with a plain little thing like that, of course, so don't you worry. He'll never likely see her again. It seems he was interested in her because he saw her at a symphony concert and saw how interested she was in music. That's his line, you know, music and uplift and all that. He would be interested in a girl who was trying to uplift herself, you see, purely from a philanthropic point of view, that's his line, Isabel, that's his line."

"Yes, and that's her line, too, Uncle Rad. She always was poking around trying to learn something more about everything. Nobody thought anything of her in school, she was a regular grind. She wasn't in the least popular. Of course, we had to be nice to her because she was in our classes, but she never was really taken in among the girls. Only now and then to speak to her about the lessons or something like that."

"Yes," spoke up Aline who was riding home in the Radnor car, and who was noted for always saying the wrong thing. "She used to do all our algebra problems for us, didn't she, Isabel? I remember once——"

But Isabel gave her a warning dig in the ribs and went loudly on:

"She used to be the most demure little thing. I never dreamed she'd develop into a man-hunter. But I'm done with her from now on, and I'll take care everybody knows just what she is."

But Isabel Cresson had yet to discover that perhaps she had but just begun with the young woman in question.

Chapter X

THE DISHES WERE FINISHED in about half the time it usually took to do them, for the helper proved most efficient.

Marion closed and locked the cupboards and handed the key to the janitor with a feeling of elation that was utterly new to her. She felt like a little girl who was going out to play.

They stepped out together into the starlight.

"My car is just around the corner," said Lyman. "Will you wait here till I bring it, or shall we walk?"

"Walk of course," said Marion joyously. To think of going home in a car! There had been few automobile rides in Marion's life and it seemed almost as great an event to her as a trip to Europe might have been to some people.

"Shall we go the long way or the short way? I'd like to show you a beautiful moonrise if you don't mind being a few minutes later getting home," he said.

"Oh, that will be lovely!" gasped Marion. "I have had very few rides lately, and I certainly shall enjoy it."

"I hope you will allow me to take you again soon, then." He smiled, and they whirled away into what seemed to Marion like enchantment.

They went through the park and out a little way into the country, through a suburb with lofty estates on either hand, and rolling golf green lying like dark velvet. They saw the moon rise, too, over the crest of a hill, and saw it rippling over a stream down in the valley, and Lyman told her how he had watched it rise in Switzerland once, describing the rosy glow on the snow-capped mountains until she almost held her breath with the delight of it.

And even then they were not very late coming home, for the little clock on Marion's bureau pointed only to half past twelve, and all that delight and wonder packed into one short hour since they had left the church. What a wonderful thing a high-powered car was. And Mr. Lyman wasn't a stranger in the city, after all. He had said they would ride soon again.

When she climbed the stairs to her little third-story room her cheeks were glowing and her eyes were bright.

"Oh, I mustn't, mustn't, be so happy as this!" she told herself in the mirror as she caught a glimpse of her own happy face. "It isn't right! I am making too much of a small courtesy. He is only being kind and polite. He probably saw how unpleasant those girls were being, and he wanted to make me forget it. I must realize that this doesn't mean a thing but Christian courtesy. Oh, I won't presume upon it, it was beautiful, and even if I never do see him again I shall always remember him with gratitude for the beautiful time he gave me to-night, and for the way he sort of championed me before Isabel."

"Is it wicked, I wonder, to be glad that that other girl didn't get him to-night, and that he stayed and helped me?" she asked herself slowly. "I don't begrudge her the nice times she has; but she has so many of them, and I had just this one. No, that isn't true, either. I just will not be ungrateful."

She went to a pretty little box on her bureau and peeped in at the shrivelled rose-leaves lying in rich heaps; and a soft fragrance stole out and sweetened the air. There were a great many beautiful things in her life, for which she was deeply thankful; and she would just take this beautiful evening, and enjoy the memory of it, shutting out all the disagreeable part, and remembering only that which was pleasant.

But sleep did not come quickly to her eyes that night despite the fact that she was very tired. Every experience of the wonderful evening had been gone over, again and again. She thrilled anew with the delight of having some-one care to stay and help her and talk to her, and lived again the beautiful ride.

She told herself many times that she just simply must not let this bit of attention turn her head or make her discontented with her simple life. She would read and study the harder so that, if ever another opportunity came of talking with anyone like Mr. Lyman, she would be better able to do it. Then there was the last concert of the season to look forward to, and it promised to be the best of all. All together, the world was a happy place, and she was glad to be in it. Yet underneath it all ran the pleasant consciousness of Lyman's last words to her. He had hoped that they might meet soon again. Did he really mean it? It seemed as if he did. And would they ever meet? When and where would there ever be an opportunity?

But her harmless little triumph was but for the night. The next morning about eleven o'clock Isabel Cresson sailed down upon her, clad in a stunning fur coat, with orchids for a boutonniére and demanded to see her in a loud, imperative voice.

Marion rose from the seat behind her special counter where she was fashioning some exquisite pink satin petals for a shoulder rose for a well-dressed woman who stood waiting, and greeted Isabel with a courteous smile. She had a premonition that Isabel meant no good in coming thus to her, but while she was not over cordial there was a sweet dignity about her that seemed to command respect.

Marion still held the lovely pink folds of ribbon in her fingers and the needle was partly pulled through a stitch. There was that about her attitude that showed Isabel that she had no time to waste, so Isabel plunged in regardless of listeners, not even troubling to hush her voice. She spoke haughtily, as to one beneath her, and more than that, as if she had the right to talk, the right of a near friend or relative.

"I just came in to wahn you, Marion, foah yoah own good," she began. "You can't get away with the stuff you put ovah last evening. It won't go down."

There was a curious blending of loftiness and modern slang in her speech. But having got under way she forgot her practised accent. She raised her voice and became a little more explicit:

"You know you can't expect people like those over in that church not to gossip, and, of course, *everybody* noticed you. I was so *ashamed* for you I didn't know what to do, to make yourself so conspicuous and fairly fling yourself at a young man like that. Of course, he's a gentle-

106

man and couldn't do a thing but be polite, or you'd have soon found out your mistake. And, of course, you know a young man in his position couldn't show attention to a girl like you without making talk. It simply isn't being done. And if he did he wouldn't mean a thing by it, but I don't suppose you knew that. I thought I'd better come and tell you."

Marion had been simply frozen into dumbness by the thing that was happening to her, her smile congealed where it had been when Isabel first started her tirade. It didn't occur to her that she could do anything to stop it. It didn't occur to her to try and answer. What was there to say to such cruelties? She just stood there and grew whiter, and her eyes grew larger and darker. A little slender straight figure like a lance standing there before that avalanche of blighting words!

"You know just what kind of a girl they'll think you are! You understand, don't you? You've always posed as being so terribly good, but you don't put that over any longer. We're wise to you now, and my advice to you is——"

But Isabel got no further, for the aisle man suddenly appeared and stepped up to her politely:

"Is there anything the matter, madam, anything that we can set straight? Something about a purchase?" and Isabel looked up to see quite a crowd collecting in the offing.

For Gladys Carr, who had chanced to pass that way as Isabel's tirade began, went scowling after the aisle man and happening to find him close at hand pulled him back with her.

"It's one of these here fierce swells," she explained, "got a line of talk t'beat the band, and little Warren isn't saying a thing! Not a darned thing! You better go quick or there won't be any little Warren left." So the aisle man came at once. Marion with her quiet ways was somewhat of a relief in his busy days.

It was a delicate matter, interceding between a customer and an employee, but he was a brave man and came courageously to the front. Isabel turned upon him haughtily, and replied in a tone that was intended to suppress him and send him off apologetically:

"No, merely a personal mattah! You needn't intahfeah!" and then she turned back to Marion with a malicious glance:

"Now, you're warned, Marion, and I wash my hands if you get into any furthah trouble. But remembah! We won't stand for anothah such performance!"

Then Isabel turned regardless of the staring onlookers and sailed away with her head in the air, and her fur coat swaggering insolently behind her.

But Marion stood still where she had left her, staring blankly, the needle held in her inert hand, the rose falling from the fingers of the other hand, almost as if she had been dead. She was white as death.

It was the voice of the customer who was waiting for her rose that recalled her to her senses and saved her from the whirling feeling that threatened to take her away entirely from the world of sense:

"My dear," she said, "my dear, don't mind her! Anyone can see what she is at a glance. Such a tirade! She ought to have been arrested."

Marion suddenly came back from the borderland, and sat down, taking up her half-finished rose, and trying to set a stitch with her trembling hands.

"Never mind, Miss Warren. I wouldn't pay any attention to that," said the aisle man kindly, looking over his glasses at Marion's white face. He was an elderly man and had a young daughter of his own growing up. "If she comes back just you send for me."

Marion thanked him with her eyes, but she could not utter a word yet. Her throat seemed dry and cold. She felt numb all over.

"Who was that poor stew?" asked Gladys, making a trip past the counter as the aisle man turned away. "Some lady, I'll say! Say, M'rian, you should worry about her! She can't put anything over on any of us, we're wise to you, see? The poor fish must be blind not to know you ain't that kind of a baby! Great cats! I'd like to meet her on a dark night and teach her a few. It's my opinion she's jealous, an' that's the whole story!"

Marion lifted a grateful glance toward Gladys as she hurried away, and then turned to her customer:

"I'm so ashamed," she said, with a catch in her breath as though she were going to cry. "There wasn't—any—occasion—whatever!"

"Of course not!" said the customer sympathetically. "That was an outrageous attack. That girl ought to have been arrested. You could have her arrested, you know. You needn't be ashamed at all. If you decide to have her arrested, I'll be glad to be a witness for you. You have my address, just let me know. I shouldn't let her get away with a thing like that."

Marion sat and worked silently through the long afternoon like one crushed. She felt so humiliated that it seemed to her she never could rise again and look anybody in the face.

And all the time Isabel's cruel arraignment was going over and over in her mind and she was reviewing moment by moment the evening before and trying to see what it could have been in her conduct that had merited such an attack. Of course, she knew that she had done nothing wrong. Could it be true that people were talking about her? If so, why? Was it such an unheard of thing that a young man should be nice to a girl, even if she wasn't of his social degree? Just for one evening. And of course he couldn't be expected to know who she was. She looked nice and behaved herself, what more was necessary at a church affair where all were supposed to be brethren? But it seemed that was not enough. She should not have gone to the social. She should not have allowed anyone to speak to her. She ought not to have any good times at all, she told herself bitterly.

She tried to rise above the shock of it and be her natural self. But continually the trouble returned no matter what line of reasoning she used. What had Isabel meant, for instance, by saying "in his position," was there something peculiar about Mr. Lyman? Was he perhaps married? Or divorced? There were a great many people divorced in these days of course. Perhaps that was what Isabel meant. Of course, that might have been what made people talk if they all knew it. But if he was divorced, who had he bought the ribbon roses for? She had always supposed they were for his wife. But perhaps they were for some girl. Perhaps he had a great many girl friends. Well, why not? Most young men had. Would that then make it a sin for another girl to sit and talk with him a little while? He had only been kind, and stayed to help her afterwards. He had been sorry for the way that the other young people treated her. That was why he took her for that ride. Her cheeks burned red at the thought. What more might not Isabel have said if she had known about the ride? But of course she could not possibly have know that.

Well, she must learn a terrible lesson by this, not to have anything more to do with young men as long as she lived, not even if all the superintendents and ministers of the universe introduced her. Not even if they appeared to be angels come down to earth.

As for this Mr. Lyman, she would think no more about him. She would likely never see him again anyway, in spite of what he had said. That was only a polite way of saying good-night. Perhaps she would go to another church for a while so that she would not have to see any of the people who had been talking about her so dreadfully. Or no, that would only be to make them think she was ashamed of herself. No, she would go, quietly, as she always had gone, attend service and go home alone. Let them think what they pleased for a while. It could not really injure her. They would soon discover that it was not true, and it would be forgotten.

But as for this Mr. Lyman, she could see that he was far above her in every way, of course, cultured and travelled, and wealthy, and it were far better for her to keep out of his sight. He was likely only studying her type. Writers did that, she had read. Perhaps he was a writer. Now she had thought of it, it seemed quite to fit him. Well, she would keep entirely away from him from this time forth, and just as soon as she felt she could reasonably withdraw from the church without causing more gossip she would do so. It would come hard to leave her Sunday School class and the minister and his wife, for they were the only two real friends she was sure of in the city.

So she gradually lifted her little head like a lily that had been stricken, and was trying hard to revive, and tried to look as if nothing had happened.

The next time she saw Lyman was two days later, Sunday night after church. He had been sitting three seats behind her all the service but she had not been aware of it.

For a moment her heart beat wildly and she wondered what to do. But she could not turn and flee in the church with people coming down the aisle. If she waited in her seat that would only make her more conspicuous, and she could not go up and talk to the minister for he was down at the front door shaking hands with people. Even Mrs. Stewart was nowhere to be seen. She had no excuse but to walk out and down the aisle as everybody else was doing.

He was waiting for her in his pew with the evident intention of walking by her side, and she did not know how to prevent it. She could not walk by with downcast eyes and pretend not to see him, or know him. He had already seen the recognition in her face as their eyes met when she turned to go out of her pew. And after all, why should she not walk down the aisle by his side? Was there anything wrong in that?

At the door they came upon Isabel and her uncle talking with a group of people, and Isabel darted her a meaningful look which pierced her like an arrow. She longed to slip out the open door and run down the street away in the dark. But of course she could not do that.

She was so overwrought that she could not think of a way to dismiss Lyman, and before she realized it, he was helping her down the steps and leading her toward his car which was parked almost in front of the door.

"Oh, but I mustn't," she said shrinking away from him. "I thank you so much, but, I mustn't trouble you any more."

"But, I don't understand," he said, looking at her disappointedly. "Aren't you going home? Well, it's right on my way to drop you there, so please don't suggest trouble. It will be a pleasure."

She was too embarrassed to know what to do, and only anxious to get out of sight of the people who were streaming out of the church now, and looking in their direction. She could see Isabel coming toward the door, too, peering out. She got into the seat quickly and shrank back out of sight only anxious to end the scene, but not before Isabel had sighted her, she feared. She must find some way to let Mr. Lyman know that he could not attend her any more. She would tell him her humble origin on the way home and that would end it.

But while she was thinking about it, trying to frame a sentence which would not sound too much as if she were

111

presuming upon his slight attentions, she found herself at her own door, and she merely found words to thank him for the ride and say good-night. After all perhaps this was best. She would just stay away from the church and from every other place where he would be likely to be, and he would soon forget her.

As for herself, would anything ever make her forget this taste of another life that she had enjoyed for a brief season? Well, perhaps the time might come when the horror of what she had passed through would blow away like a death-laden fog, and she might have for her own, the memory of those interesting talks, and the glimpses into travel and literature that he had given her.

Chapter XI

FROM TIME TO TIME Monday morning, as she sat and wrought her flower work, Isabel's glance of hate recurred to her. It seemed a glance that needed thinking about. There had been recrimination in it. Marion had seemingly transgressed again, she supposed, by walking down that aisle with Lyman, although it was perfectly plain that there was nothing else for her to do unless she made a scene out of it and refused to speak to him. But what would Isabel do next? Was it conceivable that she would go to Lyman with some tale about herself? Well, she must endure that, too, perhaps. But what was all this happening to her for? She had always tried to do right. Even in this matter of staying in the city when the others went to the farm her conscience was clear. It could not be punishment for her selfishness could it?

Dr. Stewart had once preached about tests. He had said that every Christian had to be tried by fire in some way, just as steel rails were tested before they were put in a railroad, to see if they were strong enough to bear the weight that was to be put upon them. Just as bridges were tested, and steam engines, and all sorts of machinery. God tested us by hard things. Well, if she were sure that was it, she might be able to endure it better. He had promised to be near and help. The words kept coming to her: "God is faithful, who will not suffer you to be tempted above that ye are able, but will with the testing also make a way of escape, that ye may be able to bear it." And apparently the way of escape did not mean getting out of the testing entirely when it began to seem too hard, because it said, "that ye may be able to bear it." Well, if she was being tested she wanted to come through it in a way that

113

I give God the glory. She didn't want to be a miserveak failure of a Christian.

All that morning as she worked away the words kept going over in her heart, "God is faithful, God is faithful," and they comforted her.

"What makes ya so silent this morning, M'rian?" asked Gladys, lingering by her counter. "Ya ain't worried about that tough egg of a high flyer yet, are ya? She ain't worth it, M'rian. I give you my word. She can't touch you."

But just then there came a call from the velvet ribbon-counter. "Miss Warren was wanted on the 'phone," and Marion was relieved that she did not have to reply. When she returned the giddy Gladys would have forgotten all about it.

It was a strange voice on the telephone, a young man. He said he was president of the Christian Endeavor Society in her church, and he gave his name, Dick Struthers. That she knew was the name of the young man who was the present president. But the voice did not sound familiar. However, she had seldom heard Dick Struthers speak. He was a shy quiet fellow, not given to words.

The voice said that there was to be a Christian Endeavor dinner held that evening at a nice quiet little hotel, some sort of a celebration of something, he seemed vague as to what it was for. He said Mrs. Stewart, the minister's wife, had asked him to call her up and make special request that Marion Warren attend. They needed a few of the older young people along to give dignity to the affair, and Mrs. Stewart had especially wanted Marion. She would have called herself but she was just leaving with Doctor Stewart for New York to attend a wedding, and hadn't time. No, it didn't cost anything. It was paid for out of the treasury. It was to be a real nice time. Marion would go, wouldn't she? One of the boys would call for her in a car at half past six. Could she be ready then? Where would she be? At home or at the store? Well, just what was her present address, he had forgotten. No, she didn't need to go home to dress up, it wasn't a dress affair. Come right from the store if she wanted to.

When Marion returned to her ribbons, she had a troubled look. She did not want to go to that dinner. She was not in the Christian Endeavor Society now, had not been for several years, not since her mother was taken sick.

114

She did not know the members very well, but they were just boys and girls of course from fourteen up. Of course it wasn't like going among older strangers. She hated to say no when Mrs. Stewart had made it a special request, and now she was committed to it, when she would so much rather have spent the evening studying in her room. She had meant not to have anything more to do with affairs at the church, not for a long time, anyway, till gossip had been forgotten and her reputation was established again —if such a thing were possible.

But this was only boys and girls.

Well, she had promised, anyway, and it was too late to back out.

So she hurried home the minute she was free, and donned a fresher dress and smoothed her hair.

She was scarcely ready when Mrs. Nash came up to say her car was at the door. The sad old landlady patted her cheek and told her she was looking real pretty, and to have a good time, and Marion went down somehow cheered by her friendliness.

She got into the car before she noticed that there was no one in it whom she knew. There were two young men in the front seat, and she was put into the back seat with two girls swathed in long cloaks, sitting back in the shadow. They merely nodded when they were introduced and neither of them spoke a word the whole way, save to answer in monosyllables indifferently when Marion suggested that it was a pleasant evening, and that this dinner was something she had not heard about until that morning. She began to think they were a grumpy lot. The two boys continually smoked cigarettes and she could get no responses from any of them. At last she gave up the effort deciding that they were very young and embarrassed, and she lapsed into silence and her own thoughts.

They had gone a good many miles and had been travelling what she judged must be nearly three quarters of an hour when they finally drew up beside a wide rambling building set among tall trees, with what looked in the darkness like beautiful grounds around them. There were red-shaded lamps in the windows, and a sound of music and laughter came through the wide-swung door.

The young men helped the girls out and they all went inside. The look of the place bewildered Marion. It did not seem like a hotel nor yet a home, but they went up a staircase, and there was a room with many comfortable looking chairs and couches, and a piano. There were red-shaded lamps here, too. A jazz orchestra was playing, and two young people, a man and a girl, were dancing in the middle of the room. Was this the kind of thing she had been sent to guard against? Did Mrs. Stewart want her to see that none of the wild young things whom she was supposed to be chaperoning did anything unseemly for young people belonging to a church organization? Her heart sank, because she felt that she would be most in-effectual in stopping anything that anybody wanted to do if many of the society were like the two girls who had ridden with her.

Much troubled in mind she followed the young people with whom she had come, threw off her wraps in the dressing room, and turned to find the two girls who ac-companied her dressed in a most unsuitable manner. They were wearing indecently short dresses of chiffon with many sketchy floaters and draperies which did not drape, and when she saw the girls in the light they were not young, they had an old coarse look. She wondered where they came from. Some new members perhaps that the minister's wife was trying to get hold of.

They paid no attention to Marion, but went to the mir-ror and began to apply cosmetics freely. Marion went and looked out of the window at a wide stretch of dim blue hills and starry sky, and wished she had not come. This was the last, the very last social affair of that church that she would ever attend. She would tell Mrs. Stewart all about it, and then she would never go to any more things among the young people again. She felt very unhappy.

When the two young women were ready she went with them across the wide room where now were several cou-ples dancing in a way that Marion felt was not at all nice. She knew very little about dancing herself, but it seemed to her that this was some kind of super-dancing of which no one who was decent could approve.

She was glad to get across the room, and out on a long glassed-in porch set with small tables, some of which were occupied by people who were being served with food. Marion noted with startled surprise that there were wine bottles on some of the tables, and that one company of four which they passed was very loud and hilarious. One of the men looked up into her face as she went by and said insolently, "Here's my baby!" She was glad to escape into the private dining-room at the end of the glass corridor. But just as she was entering, behind the other two girls, someone came roughly out singing in a high key and jostled against her rudely, disarranging her dress as he brushed past her. She did not notice till afterward that the deep crimson ribbon rose which she had made for herself that day to brighten up her sombre little dress, had been torn from her shoulder. She was too much engaged otherwise to notice it was gone.

For the room was blue with cigarette smoke, and as she looked around in amazement, she saw that not only the men but the women also were smoking, and that she could not recognize a single face that she had ever seen before.

There were bottles on this table, too, a long table with about twenty people seated about it. They had begun to eat, or rather to drink, and were very noisy about it.

"Why, we've gotten into the wrong room," said Marion suddenly clutching at the dress of the girl who stood next to her. "Let's get out quick! This is a terrible place!"

The girl turned and gave her a wise evil leer, and suddenly a man's voice cried out in a thick unsteady voice:

"Why, there's Marry'n, little Marry'n. Precious Child! Come 'ere an' sit by me, Marry'n, pretty li'l Marry'n. Les' have a drink an' then we'll sing, 'She's my baby! Marry'n's my baby!'" His voice trailed off drunkenly, as a door at the far end of the room opened and someone came in. Marion turned wild eyes of hope toward her. She was clad in an inadequate sheathing of cloth of gold and her gold hair was bound about her forehead with a green jewelled serpent. She came steadily on toward Marion with a cold hard look in her eyes, and suddenly Marion saw that it was Isabel.

"Get her good and drunk, boys!" cried out Isabel in a tone like a scimitar, "nothing short of drunk will do. We've got to teach her a few lessons."

And suddenly Marion felt she was surrounded by these strange hilarious men, each with a glass in his hand, and she stood at bay, her back against the wall, her lips moving

117

soundlessly. The words they were speaking, without her conscious volition were:

"God is faithful, who will not suffer you above that ye are able. God is faithful! God is faithful! Oh, God! Come! Help me!" and mid the wild screams of laughter at her last words which had been audible she sank white and still to the floor.

"Yes, God'll help her a lot! She'll find out!" said Isabel, cool and steady and sneering. "Dan, hand me that glass. Did you mix it the way you said first? Now, hold up her head. I'll make her drink it. Ted, you pry open her teeth. No, lift her head higher. That's right!"

Jefferson Lyman had found the two books which he had promised Marion he would lend her. That was one of the things he had said Sunday night, which she had not taken in because she was so distraught. If she had realized that he was coming to bring her some books, she would have been more worried than ever and have felt that she must plan something more decisive than merely to be out.

But he had thought to forestall missing her by going to her boarding house about the time he thought she would reach there from the store. He had even meditated asking her to go out to dinner somewhere with him if she seemed in the mood, and had nothing else to do.

He reached the house door in his own car, just in time to see another car driving away. He remembered it because he thought he recognized the driver and wondered what he was doing in that neighborhood. As he waited at the door for his ring to be answered, he looked up the street after the car which was halted for the moment by a traffic light, and idly wondered again whose it was.

Mrs. Nash appeared at the door almost instantly for she had been watching at the parlor window to see Marion go away and had been astonished to see a second car drive up as the first left.

"No, she ain't here," she said in answer to his question. "She's just left this minute. You can catch her if you want to. They can't be far. Ain't been gone a minnit! She's gone to some kind of a Chrishun Dever spread out in the country. They came fur her. Ain't you one of their crowd? Was she expectin' you?"

But Lyman, with a sudden intuition had excused himself and was back in his car before she had finished her sentence. "My land but he's short!" said Mrs. Nash aloud to herself. "But he's better lookin' than the other one. I kinda wisht she'd waited fur this one."

Lyman sprang into his car and threw in the clutch. The lights had changed and the car ahead leaped on with a jerk and was rounding the next corner. Lyman dashed after it.

During that long hard ride in pursuit of the car ahead, Lyman wondered at himself. Why was he doing this? In the first place he wasn't altogether certain that he had followed the right car. In the gathering dusk with the crowded condition of traffic in the city there had been two or three turnings when he was not sure he was following the right speck of ruby light. And now since they were out on the lonely highway, though he had sprinted forward several times to get a good look at the car, his quarry had also started up madly and torn along at a pace that worried him. The road they were taking as well as the speed they were making perplexed him. And it seemed altogether ridiculous to suppose that the quiet little Marion Warren would be riding with people who drove like that. Of couse, if it were some young boy who was driving—but somehow his conviction kept him going even against his better sense.

That they should have turned in at the road house where they finally arrived, was altogether fitting with Lyman's instincts for that car, but by this time, he had decided that he was a fool, and that, of course, Marion Warren would not be in that car. She was probably at this minute sitting around some quiet pleasant table partaking of a homely supper of cold ham and Saratoga potatoes and pickles and cake and canned peaches. It was absurd that he should make such a fool of himself, and probably get into a mix-up and maybe see someone that he would rather not have recognize him in a place like this. He would go back. As soon as he had a good look at that car to make sure that his first guess about its owner was right, he would turn around and go back. He would not try to go in on so slender a chance as the mere hunch that he thought he had.

But when he had confirmed his suspicions about the car, some inner light drew him further. Now that he was here he would be sure. He saw another car on the edge of the parking space that gave him another idea. Drunken men were not to be trusted. At least, if Marion Warren were in such a place and such company of her own free will he wanted to know the truth before he went any farther in his acquaintance. He was going in rather for what he hoped he would not find than for what he would.

So he went inside.

"Got any private dinners on to-night, Jack?" he asked casually of the proprietor who stood about respectably and eyed him.

"One or two." He eyed the newcomer up and down and clamped his lips shut.

"Atkins here?" he hazarded.

A knowing gleam responded and a slight lifting of the left eyebrow. "You belong to the crowd?" The proprietor was a bit doubtful.

"I'll just go up. Want to see him in a hurry."

"First room beyond the balcony," murmured the proprietor and turned on his heel. If it wasn't all right he didn't want to know anything about it.

"Is this a practical joke or a case of kidnapping for the police?" asked a cool incisive voice above the wild babel in the room beyond the glass corridor.

There was instant silence, and a stealthy melting away toward the door at the far end of the room. When Lyman raised his eyes to ask for a glass of water there was no one else in the room but Marion lying white and still on the floor where she had fallen. Had he seen Isabel Cresson but an instant before in a golden garment that left bare the greater portion of her back—or was it only a figment of his imagination?

He reached for a glass of water from the table and dashed it into the unconscious girl's face. Then as he saw her eyelids quiver he gathered her up in his arms and carried her rapidly down the corridor, across the deserted dance floor, and out the door to his car. The tables were strangely free from bottles as he passed them, though he might not have noticed them had there been ten thousand, and all the people who sat about eating were decorously sober. The other rooms were entirely empty and he did not see the proprietor anywhere about, but he did not stay to hunt for him. He laid Marion gently in the back seat and drove like mad toward the city.

Half-way back she came to herself fully and sat up, more frightened than ever to find herself moving through the darkness at such a rapid rate. Had her tormentors taken her yet further from her home? Was there no help anywhere? Wouldn't it be better to risk opening the door softly and jumping out rather than to stay and take what might be ahead? Her nerves were so unstrung that she could not think.

But Lyman became aware of her almost instantly and turning reassured her.

"Lie still, Marion," he said gently. He called her Marion and did not know it. She held her breath in wonder. Was she ill, or dreaming? How could he have possibly have come here?

"You are perfectly safe. Just close your eyes and try to rest. You are all right. Don't try to think about anything, yet."

After a moment of wonder she asked him in a faint voice:

"How did you come to be there?"

"I didn't come to be there," he answered grimly. "I don't frequent such places. But I didn't like the way your driver was curving all over the road and I came to find out if you were there. Your landlady told me you were in the car."

She was silent a moment and then she said in an awed voice, "Then He did help. He was faithful!"

Lyman considered this a moment before he asked:

"Just who are you talking about?"

"God!" said Marion, a ring of triumph in her voice.

"Yes," said Lyman reverently, "He did. I didn't know what made me keep going on against my better judgment, but I guess that was it."

"And I can never thank you!" she exclaimed, remembering how she had planned never to see him again. What if he had not come?

"Don't try," he said lightly. "You've come through too much, and so have I."

"But I don't understand how you knew I was there? Did anyone tell you?"

"No, I just had a hunch, as they say. I went in to make sure you were not there, and when I got to a closed door with a regular fracas going on behind it, I almost turned back. It was this made me open the door and there you were!"

To her amazement he laid a little crushed satin rose in her lap.

"My rose!" she exclaimed in wonder, "I must have lost if off my dress when that man pushed past me!"

She dropped back wearily on the cushion, looking white and spent. "Don't talk!" he commanded, "you've had a shock. You need a rest!" He was gravely silent, almost tender as he helped her out of the car, but when he left her with the command to go straight to sleep and not think about the affair, she found Mrs. Nash waiting for her in the front hall.

"Well, you came back with the right fella, anyhow," she said with satisfaction. "I didn't like that first fella you went off with at all."

'No," said Marion decidely, "I didn't either, and I shall never go with him again if I can help it."

"Well, I'm glad this other man found ya. He was powerful disappointed when he found you had gone. You'd oughtta waited fur him. He's real nice."

"I didn't know he was coming," said Marion softly, looking down at the two books he had left in her hand at parting. But when she went up to her room and sat down to face the situation, her eyes began to fill with horror, and her cheeks to burn. It had suddenly occurred to her that perhaps he thought she had gone to that awful place of her own free will. As she recalled his constrained manner, his reserved, almost distant tone, his silence, her agitation grew. Oh, why had she not explained fully? How could she bear to have him think that of her?

She tried to sleep, but could not. Perhaps she would never have another opportunity to explain. Sometime in the night she began to pray: "Dear Lord, I put this all in your hands, to straighten out as you see fit. I guess I've been an awful fool!" Then peace descended and she slept.

Chapter XII

WITH ALL THE EXCITEMENT that had been going on Marion had almost lost sight of the thrill she usually felt in wondering whether there would be another rose in her chair at the next concert. She went early, however, that last night, because she wanted to enjoy every minute from the time the doors were opened. There would be a long summer without these wonderful breaks in the monotony of work, and she must store it all up to help her through the heat and weariness.

Slowly she climbed the stairs, trying not to think it was the last time this year, glancing in as she passed the empty balcony and boxes where the favored great would come later to lend their countenance and costumes to the evening for a little while, and wondering as she had done many times before how it would seem to belong in that velvet grandeur always, instead of up in the highest gallery.

Softly she trod the deep carpet of the hallway, and went down the steps to her chair, and there, yes, there lay *two roses*! Two wonderful great crimson buds! There had never been two before.

She looked hurriedly around. There was no one on that floor yet, and no one in the audience-room that she could see from where she stood, except a man up in the top box next to the stage. He was almost hidden by the heavy crimson hangings of the box, and he seemed to be studying the fresco work of the ceiling through an opera glass. He seemed as far away from her as a man in Mars might be. She stooped and caught the rosebuds to her face, and kissed them and whispered: "Oh, you dear things! You *dear* things! You lasted all the way through, didn't you?"

With a quick glance behind her to be sure no one had come in yet, and with the roses still caught to her heart, she made a tiny graceful curtsey and a wave of her free hand toward the great empty room, whispering softly: "I thank you! I thank you!" It seemed as if her full heart must give some expression to her feelings; and, as she knew no one to thank, she threw her little grateful rejoicing out into the wide universe, trusting that it would somehow be brought home to its rightful owner.

Then she nestled down quietly in her seat, with the roses fastened in her dress. They seemed to soothe away all the pain of the past weeks with their soft, cool fragrance, and make her happy again. At least she would forget all her perplexities for this one night and enjoy everything to the full. She had ceased to wonder where they came from. They were the more beautiful that they were a mystery. She shrank from the thought of finding out their donor, most lest it should bring her disappointment of some kind.

She sat in a dream of joy as one by one the people stole in and the orchestra began to tune their instruments. It seemed to her as if this too were a part of the beauty of the evening, as if these magicians of harmonies were calling together one by one each note and theme and melody, like sweet, reluctant spirits that together were presently to bring forth divine harmonies.

She took little notice of anyone around her that night. The roses and the music were enough. She wanted to take it all in and seal it up for memory's serving in the days of music-famine that were almost upon her.

With the little black hat in her lap, and the deep burning roses nestling at her breast, where their glow was reflected upon the whiteness of her sweet face, she sat with closed eyes and shapely dark head covered with shining ripples, leaning back against the crimson of the high-backed chair. She listened as if she were out in a tide of melody, floating, floating with the melody where it would, her soul palpitating, quivering, feeling every suggestion the music conveyed, seeing every fair picture that it carried on its breath.

Down in a box below sat Isabel Cresson attired in a

costly gown, several diamonds much in evidence. She was gazing through an exquisitely mounted pair of opera glasses. She was cross with all the people who sat about her, for she had searched every spot in the floor and lower balcony for a certain man, and found him not; and then she had turned her attention reluctantly to the rest of the house and found him not, because a broad woman with a towering hat completely hid him from her view. But she found with her powerful lenses the vision of a sweet face leaning back and listening with closed eyes, above two exquisite crimson rosebuds. Rosebuds which she knew could be found only at the best florists'. It vexed her beyond endurance, and she heard not a note of that whole wonderful concert. Perhaps, however, she had not come to listen. For she had been most uneasy in her mind ever since the road house episode. Just how much did Jefferson Lyman see in that inner room? Did he know she had been there? She would have given her best diamond to find out.

The last sweet note died away, and the musicians had stolen out one by one before Marion put on her hat with a happy sigh and turned to go, taking a deep breath of her roses as she bent her head.

Then she raised her eyes, and there he stood, tall and smiling before her, just in front of the chair where the man had sat that she had noticed once or twice; and with a gasp of astonishment she suddenly realized that it had been he all the time.

And she had wondered who it was he resembled!

He smiled down into her eyes with that deep understanding that made her heart quiver with a glad response and caused her to forget all her nice little resolutions and phrases.

He was just a part of the wonder of it all that night, and the air was still athrob with the music that he and she had both been in, and lived through, and understood. Its heartbreaks and its ecstasies were their common experience, and there could be no question of their right to talk it over and feel anew the thrill of the evening's pleasure.

"It was without a flaw to-night, was it not?" he said as he bent courteously to assist her up the steps, and somehow that low-spoken sentence seemed to bring all the symphony nights into one and make them theirs. She forgot she had not meant to let him take her home again.

They were talking of the music, comparing one selection with another, calling attention to the exquisite pathos of one passage, or the magnificent climax of another; and so, before Marion had realized it, they were on her shabby door-step, and all the words she had planned were left unsaid.

"I want to explain about last Tuesday," she said earnestly. "I did not know those awful people, nor where I was going. I got a telephone message that Mrs. Stewart wanted me to chaperon a Christian Endeavor party, and they would call for me."

He looked at her with something in his eyes that thrilled her. "Of course," said he, "I understood as soon as I saw who they were. There ought to be some way to bring them to justice, but let's forget them for the present.

"Is it ever possible for you to get away from the store on Saturday afternoons?" It was the first time he had hinted that he knew she was in the store. He knew, then, that she had to work for her living!

"Why—I—yes, I suppose I could," she found herself saying. "Yes, I think I could.. I haven't asked any time off; we are entitled to a few days during the year."

"Well, then suppose you try for next Saturday afternoon. I have tickets for a recital which I am sure you will enjoy. It promises to be far finer than anything we have had among the soloists this winter. It is Paderewski, the great pianist. Have you ever heard him?"

"Oh!" She caught her breath. "Oh, no! I have never heard him, but I have read of him a great many times. He is very wonderful, more than all the others, isn't he? You have heard him?"

"Yes," he said smiling, "I have heard him, here and abroad; and I think he is the greatest. There are people who criticize him, but then there are those who would criticize that!" He waved his hand toward the brilliant bit of night that hung over the street, a wonderful dark azure path between the rows of tall houses, luminous with a glorious silver moon and studded with myriads of stars.

She looked up, and understood, and then met his

126

glance with delighted comprehension. She knew that he felt she would understand.

"Oh, thank you!" she said. "I hope I can get away. It would be the greatest pleasure I can think of to hear him."

He looked into the depths of her eyes for an instant and exulted in their starry shine. She seemed so utterly sweet and natural.

"Then shall we arrange for it, unless I hear from you that you cannot get away?" he asked. "And may I call for you here, or will some other place be more convenient?"

"I could not get away until the last minute," she said thoughtfully. "There would not be time to come home, I'm afraid; and, dear me! I'll not be very fine to go to a concert straight from the store without a chance to freshen up."

"You always look nice," he said, admiringly. "Then suppose I meet you in the Chestnut Street waiting-room at half past two. Will that be quite convenient, or is there some other place you would prefer?"

Before she realized it was all settled, he was gone, and she was on her way up to the little room at the top of the house.

But somehow in spite of her happiness over her coming pleasure there seemed to be an undertone of self-accusation in her heart. She had not revealed her station in life to him thoroughly, and she ought to have done so. Even though he did know she was working in a store for the present, he might think it was on account of some sudden reverse of fortune, and that because Mr. Radnor had introduced her among other girls she must necessarily have come of a fine old family, and be a girl of education and refinement. The dull old wall-paper on the hall seemed to cry out "Shame!" to her as she passed by; the very cheap pine stair banisters mocked her with their bony spindles, and reminded her that he thought her more than she was, and she had not undeceived him.

"He has not been in this shabby house," they seemed to say. "He does not know how you live in poverty. If he could see us all as we are, we, your surroundings, he would never be inviting you to go to grand concerts. He will only turn your head, and make you discontented, and then when he finds out—*when he finds out*—WHEN HE FINDS OUT!" They fairly shouted it through the keyhole at her as she shut her door sharply and lighted her gas, trying to solace her troubled mind with a glimpse of the dainty refuge she had made.

She tried to forget these things in looking at her roses as she unpinned them before her glass, and laid them tenderly on the white bed-spread.

"You dears!" she said, "if you could only last till next Saturday, but you won't. And you're the very last. There'll be no more chances for you any more. Bless the dear old lady, whoever she is"—she had settled it long ago that the donor of the roses was a dear old lady with white hair, like the one who sat in the balcony below and sometimes looked up in her direction, and who probably sent her servant up to leave the rose in her seat. She never troubled any more to explain just how or why. It was like a sweet fairy tale which one took on faith—"The dear old lady will never know where to find me any more; at least, unless I get the same seat next year; and I'm afraid that is not possible, for they told me the former holder wanted it again next year. Perhaps, now, perhaps—that's an idea. What if somebody has been putting flowers in that former owner's seat, and doesn't know she is gone away? Maybe they have been meant for her all the time. Well, she was off to Europe or somewhere, and I have enjoyed the roses for her. If I had not, they might have withered unnoticed. But isn't it great, great, *great* that I'm to hear the real Pader—how *did* he pronounce that name? I wonder? I must listen when he speaks it again, and remember just how it was."

Thus communing with herself she managed to silence for a time the voices of her poverty that were crying out against her. But, when she was alone upon her pillow in the dark, once more her conscience arose, and reminded her that she did not know a thing about this stranger save that he was kind. Of course, Mr. Radnor had introduced him, and also the minister, who had seemed very fond of him, but they did not expect her to go trailing off everywhere with him, and mercy— he might be married! Married men nowadays did sometimes pay attention to girls. But she was not that kind of a girl. She resolved that she would tell him all about herself plainly the next time she saw him. Perhaps it would be after church to-morrow night; and, if it was, she would be brave and tell him quickly before he could make her fear to lose the joy of that wonderful concert.

She might, of course, wait for just this one more great pleasure; to go to a real concert with a man like that would be a thing to remember all one's life. But, if one took a forbidden pleasure what could there be in the memory but shame and bitterness?

There was no way but to tell him all about it at once. If he did not come to church Sunday evening, perhaps she ought to write him a note, and decline to go to the concert. But then that would seem to be making so much of the whole matter, as if she were taking his small attentions too seriously. What should she do? Oh for her dear father to advise her! He had not been highly educated, nor much used to the ways of the world; but somehow he had always seemed to possess a keen sense to know what to do on every occasion, and his love for his one daughter had made him highly sensitive to help her on all occasions.

Between her joy over the prospective pleasure and her worrying over this matter she had a week of most intense excitement. Sometimes she thought she would send him word that she could not go, without explaining anything; and sometimes she thought she would go for this once and have her good time, telling him afterward. Once more could do no harm. And yet in spite of all her questionings she went steadily forward with her preparations.

Her problem was by no means solved by the fact that Lyman did not appear in church Sabbath evening, and that early Monday morning a note was brought to her door from him, saying that he had found a telegram awaiting him the evening before, which had called him away from the city immediately, not to return until Friday evening; but he hoped that she would arrange matters satisfactorily for the concert on Saturday, for he was counting on the pleasure of her company.

When she opened the envelope, her heart gave a wild throb of pleasure. It was so wonderful to be receiving notes like other girls, so marvellous that he cared to be kind to her!

Yet it troubled her and frightened her to think she cared so much. If her dear father were with her, she felt certain he would warn her against losing her heart to this man. It was out of the question that he could be her intimate friend, so far apart they were in everything. If her father had lived, and she could have gone on with her studies, it might have been possible in time that she could have been fitted to be a worthy friend of such a one.

She sighed, and pressed back the tears that smarted in her eyes. She would not give up to discontent. She would take this one pleasure yet, this concert. It was too late now to stop it. He had given her no address except his home, and he was to be away all the week. It was not quite polite to send a refusal at the last minute when perhaps he could get no one else to accompany him, though of course he could probably always get good company. There was no sense in blinding herself; she might just as well admit that she was weak enough to want this one more real pleasure before she stopped altogether her friendliness with the only worthy man who had ever sought her out and seemed to care for her company. She would go to the concert, and then on the way home she would briefly and quietly tell him all about herself. That would end it. It were better ended before her whole life was spoiled with useless longing for a companionship that could never be hers. She must stop it before it was too late, and save herself.

Yet the tears that wet her pillow that night ought to have made her doubt whether it was not already too late.

That noon she took time from her lunch-hour to hover about the remnant-counters and make a few modest purchases, and that evening she began to evolve a charming little afternoon dress for herself modelled after one in the French department, a blouse from a remnant of silk and a bit of chiffon she had bought. Marion was skilful with her needle, and she had wonderful imported creations to copy. The dress was an exquisite triumph of art when completed, and fitted her admirably besides being most becoming.

Browsing around in the millinery department, she discovered a table of last year's hats, and among them a very fine imported one whose brim was slightly damaged; and the price was merely nominal. The artist in the girl saw the possibilities in that hat. She bought it at once, and that night remedied the defect by a deft bit of trimming. The result was most charming.

"If I only had some of those wonderful roses," she sighed. "I should really look quite grand for once." But of course there would be no more roses.

The new dress and the pretty hat went to the store next morning, the dress in a small pasteboard box. Marion appeared in her place behind the counter in her plain dress as usual, and only her shining eyes like two stars, and the soft flush on her cheek, told that anything unusual was to happen that day.

About eleven o'clock there appeared at the ribbon-counter a boy with a large box asking loudly for Miss Warren. Marion was making ribbon-violets for a fussy old lady, patiently trying to please her, and did not notice the boy; but the other girls were not oblivious. They brought the box to her in great excitement.

"That's the boy from Horton's!" said one girl. "Say M'rion Warren, you must have a swell friend to send you flowers from that place. Seems to me you keep it mighty quiet."

But Marion only smiled at them, and laid the box on the floor beside her. "Thank you," she said, and went on making her violets quite as if she had expected this box, though her fingers were trembling and her face had grown white with excitement. Could it be that the box contained more roses? Could it be that someone really knew her and was sending them to her? Yes, it must be, for this was the second time they had come in a box and directly from a florist.

She had never been able to explain the other time, the day after she had come home in the rain and caught cold. But now she must face the question that she had been putting aside. Who could be sending her flowers?

It was someone who knew her actions, who cared when she was ill, and who knew she was going to a concert. No one knew that but her old landlady who had happened up to the door while she was making her new dress. She had showed her the hat and dress, and told her that a friend had invited her to go to a concert. But that poor old lady would never have thought of lovely roses, even if she had desired to do something pleasant; and she certainly never could have afforded them. What was Marion to think?

It had never occurred to her to connect the roses with her new friend. They were part of her life before he came into it, and of course he could not have sent them. She would have been too humble to think such a thing possible.

But the rest of the morning she worked in a tremor of delicious excitement. She slipped the box, unopened, under the lower shelf, and went on with her ribbons, much to the disappointment of the other girls, who wanted a glimpse of what it contained. But she could not bear to open it before them all.

However, at half past one, when she was excused for the day, she hurried up to the privacy of the small dressing-room set aside for employees; and, finding that the box contained far more roses than she could possibly wear at once, she hurried back with her arms full of lovely buds, and bestowed one on each of her comrades.

"I don't care," said one of the loudest-voiced of them all, after they had thanked her, and she had slipped away again, "I don't care! I think she's just a sweet little thing, if she is awful quiet and close about herself. She deserves to have nice friends. She's different somehow from most folks, and she seems to fit those roses. I'm glad she's got the afternoon off, even if I do have to look after some of her customers. She was awful good to me when I had the grippe, and I hope she has a good time with her roses and her swell friends."

"Yes, she's all right," assented another girl, burying her nose deep in her rose. And the others all chorused, "Sure, she is!" as they separated to their various places, each breathing the perfume of her rose.

Marion ate no lunch. She was too much excited. The great hour was here at last, and after it would come the time of self-humiliation. But she was going to forget all about it until the concert was over. She was going to enjoy to the full the joy that had been set before her.

She hurried to the dressing-room, and donned the new dress and hat. The old dress was tucked away in the box to stay in her locker until Monday.

She thought with a qualm of conscience as she turned away from the glass that perhaps she ought not to have made herself look quite so much like a girl of his own class, and then the task before her would have been easier.

It seemed very strange to her to sit in a luxurious chair in the waiting-room, dressed like a lady, and see the whirl of life go on about her, while off in the distance she could glimpse the ribbon-counter, with the girls going busily about, now and then stopping to smell their roses. A happy smile came into Marion's eyes as she noticed this, and she bowed her face to her own glorious roses fastened on her breast. She was glad over the roses, that they had come that special day in time for the concert, and that there had been enough to give the other girls some, the other girls, who were not going to have her good time. She wished she might thank the giver.

He came exactly on the minute appointed; and, when she stood up quietly at his approach, he half paused and caught his breath at the lovely vision she made, the soft cream-colored dress, the becoming hat, the shining of her eyes, the glow of her cheeks above the velvet of the gorgeous roses. He had not known how beautiful she was before, he told himself, though he had always thought her lovely. Did the roses, or the clothes, or the joy in her face, make all that difference, wondered he? How he should like to spend his life making her look like that!

Chapter XIII

A SWEET SHYNESS came down upon Marion as they went on their way to the Academy of Music. Her companion seemed to see and understand, and he did most of the talking himself, making her forget the strangeness of it all.

But when they entered the Academy by the great front door where only the select who frequented the boxes might enter she was filled with awe.

They mounted only one low flight of broad marble stairs, and entered the enchanted precincts of the first balcony; and he led her to one of the luxurious boxes in the semi-circle, set apart by crimson curtains. When she sank into her velvet chair down close to the front rail, and looked out over the great room, and down upon the platform that she had before seen only from afar, she realized that everything was different from this point of view.

For an instant her soul quivered before the thought that her other world where she belonged, which was represented by the highest gallery, would perhaps be spoiled for her by this brief stay in luxury. Then she put it all aside joyously. Never mind if her own world seemed not so grand by contrast. She would always know hereafter how it felt to be one of those favored ones down here. She was having her taste of the delights of luxury, and she would enjoy concerts all the more after having this broader view of life.

Sitting thus with the crimson background, the crimson roses against the soft tan of her dress, Marion was beautiful. Isabel Cresson, on the other side of the house in a gloomy proscenium box, attended by her aunt, was unable to recognize her. There was nothing about her costume that could be criticized. It had the stamp of a foreign maker just because the owner had caught the cunning of the great originators of her models.

Isabel was baffled by the sight and much disquieted within her. She studied the other girl again and again through the afternoon; but not once did she dream that she was the plain, despised Marion Warren, sitting in the seat of the mighty and looking as lovely as one of them. She tried once to signal Lyman to bring his friend around to meet her; but he did not seem to see her, and she had to solace herself with watching his devotion to his beautiful companion.

From the moment when the great pianist came to the platform until the last lingering note of the last encore was over, and the last bow was received with jubilant applause, Marion was utterly unconscious of self. The strong, fine personality of the musician, which seemed to fill the great auditorium and dominate every being in it from the moment of his entrance, charmed her.

Marion's heart swelled with wonder at the miracle of the music. No player or players, no singer or instrument, had ever affected her quite as this great man did.

She listened with her soul in her eyes as the master fingers struck the keys, and the instrument responded as if it were glad of the hand that touched it. The music seemed to drip from his finger-tips like liquid jewels flashing as they fell. The young untaught girl drank it in most eagerly, forgetting everything besides; and the man who had brought her forgot to listen in watching her keen delight. The great master of the keys might be at his best, and at another time this man would have rejoiced in it; but to-day the music was but a lovely setting for his love, which shone like priceless pearls amidst it all.

After the programme was over they called the pianist back, seven, eight times; and each time he played again as if he could not bear to deny them the gift to which they had accorded so great applause. When at last he was gone, and the reluctant audience came down to earth again and began to pick up their belongings, Marion turned to her companion with a radiant face and a sigh of ecstasy.

"Oh, it has been like being in heaven for a little while and hearing someone who had learned of God."

"Perhaps he has," said Lyman reverently. "It seems as if no other man could so nearly reach our ideals of the heavenly music."

"I shall remember it always," said the girl, her eyes shining like two stars.

Then suddenly, as they passed from the hall into the thronged street, she realized that it was over, and her task-time had come.

She must tell him. But all the simple speech she had fashioned took flight, and left her trembling so that she tottered as she went down the wide stone steps to the pavement; Lyman put out his hand, and steadied her courteously.

"You have no call to hurry home, have you?" he said. "Suppose we go somewhere and have dinner together. I always like to talk it out after hearing a concert like that, and I want to know your impressions."

"That would be beautiful," she waid wistfully; "but I oughtn't to. I must go right home, I think."

Because he had very much set his heart upon this little dinner together, and would be greatly disappointed not to have it, he urged her.

"Oh, why? Is someone expecting you? Have you promised?"

"Oh, no!" she answered quickly. "No, there is no one, but——"

"But what? Can't you give me this little pleasure? I had quite counted on it, you see—but perhaps I should have told you beforehand. Of course, if it isn't convenient——"

"Oh, no!" she said desperately. "It's not anything like that, and it's very kind of you to ask me, and to say it would be a pleasure to you; but——"

"Well, it *would* be a pleasure, a great, big pleasure," he said pointedly; and she felt that there was something more than ordinary feeling behind the words. Then she plunged blindly in.

"It's just that I felt that I have been having too good a time lately, and I must stop it, or I shall be spoiled. You see I'm not used to many good times, and I might get very much discontented with my life." She stumbled along, hardly knowing what she was saying; and he smiled

136

indulgently down into her face, and drew her arm gently within his own in a protecting way as they came to the street-crossing, guiding her skilfully between the crowding, impatient motor-cars that were huddled in the street.

"I'd like a chance to spoil you a little," he said, and his voice was very tender. The glance of his eyes even in the electric glow of the street made her heart stand still, as if she looked into a mighty joy upon which she must herself shut the door.

"Oh, but you don't understand!" she said desperately. "It's very kind and nice, and it's been so beautiful, but I ought to have told you before. I ought not to have let you think——" She paused, unable to find words; and another congested street-crossing interrupted their conversation for a moment. She never noticed that he was guiding her steps toward the region of the better class of downtown tea-rooms and restaurants. She was not familiar with these places, and would never have thought of it if she had noticed.

"Let me think what, please?" he asked gravely when they were safe on the other side of the street. His own heart was beating hard now. Was she going to tell him that she had a lover somewhere struggling to earn enough for her support, and that she could not accept his attentions any longer? His hand trembled as he laid it upon her little gloved one that rested on his arm so lightly.

"I have let you think I'm just like those other girls you know.".

"Oh, you're mistaken about that," he answered quickly. "I never thought you were like them. Thank God you are not. If you had been, I should not have cared to have your company. You knew that the first night at the church reception."

"Oh, that is not it, either," she said desperately. It seemed so very hard to make him understand. And she felt a great sob swelling up through her throat. What should she do when it arrived?

"Look here," he said, and his voice was very peremptory; "tell me this." He paused at the corner, and detained her a little out of the crowd of passers. "Just tell me this one thing. Do you belong to someone else? Is there any reason why it is not right for you to go with me to-night?"

"Oh, no," she gasped, almost laughing, "there isn't anyone at all. I don't belong to anyone in the whole wide world any more, and there's nobody belongs to me except my brother Tom and his family; but they have each other, and they haven't time to think about me. I certainly am making a terrible mess of telling you, and you will think I am very stupid to make so much out of it all; only I've enjoyed it so much, and I knew I ought to explain it for your sake."

"There!" said Lyman, laughing joyously, and drawing her onward again. "There; don't say another word about it till we've had something to eat. If there isn't anyone else, I'm sure what you have to say won't matter in the least. Anyway, it can wait until we're out of the crowd."

He guided her carefully through the maze of people hurrying hither and yon away from business or pleasure to their homes and dinners. All the time his strong, firm hand was held close over her little, trembling one, steadying and seeming to want to comfort and reassure her; and in a moment more he led her into a great, brilliant room lined with palms and set with little tables where snowy linen, glittering glass and silver, and delicate china glowed under the warm light of rosy candle-shades. Low-voiced men and women were seated here and there conversing while a sweet-stringed orchestra, concealed, somewhere not too near by, sent forth delicious sounds like some sweet, subtle perfume filling the air.

He seated her at one of the little tables in a far corner, where a screen of palm half hid them from the room and yet revealed its beauties to them. She felt as if she were suddenly plunged into a wonderful fairy-land where she had no right to be, yet could not get away. Delight and distress were struggling for the mastery in her face, and the pretty color came and went, making her more vividly beautiful than he had ever seen her yet. He looked at her with deep satisfaction and admiration as he hung up his coat and seated himself opposite to her.

"I wonder what you like," he said, smiling. "May I try and see if I can please you?"

"Oh, anything!" she said, embarrassed. What would he think of her way of ordering, always looking at the figures in the right-hand column of the menu first to pick out the cheapest viands, and then choosing from those?

With the ease of one accustomed, Lyman took up the menu, and, running down the list, in a low voice rapidly mentioned what he wanted to the deferential waiter, who seemed to understand at once, and vanished, leaving them alone.

"Now," said Lyman, "If you will feel better to tell me at once, I will listen. What is it that you thought I ought to know?" His kindly eyes were upon her, and the color flamed into her cheeks until they rivalled the roses at her breast.

"I think you ought to know that I am a very poor girl, who has to earn my own living—and————" She paused for more words.

"I surmised as much," said he; "did you think I was mercenary, that I had to choose my friends from among wealthy people only?"

"Oh, no," she said in great distress. "You do not understand yet! I am not only poor, but I am uneducated. I have had very few opportunities. I have never been to college. All those other girls have."

He laughed.

"Why, I have been to college myself; and I'm not so sure that I'm much better off for it, either. The fact is, I fooled much of my time away in college, and learned more outside afterwards. I hadn't learned what college was for before I went, perhaps. As for those other girls, I doubt if Isabel Cresson is the wiser for her college course. I myself heard her tell a woman, a friend of mine, that all she went for was to get into the sororities. She could not possibly have enjoyed that music as you did this afternoon.

But Marion was struggling with her task. How could she overcome his great kindness and make plain to him what she meant?

"Thank you," she said gently; "but there is something she has which I have not, and which must always be a great lack in the eyes of everybody. She comes of a fine old family, and she has culture and refinement behind her. She is used to going among people. She knows how to move and speak and act. My father was a plain mechanic. He worked in the Houghton Locomotive Works. We were not so very poor while he lived, because he earned good wages. He meant to give me a good education. That was

139

what he wanted above everything else, but he died before he was able to accomplish it. He was only a mechanic, but he was a good man and a dear father——"

"I know," said Lyman gently. "He had the accident from which he died through doing a kindness for another man who was in trouble. I have stood beside his own machine at Houghton's and heard the foreman tell the whole story. He described the scene when your father was found hurt, and they were about to take him home. He said there wasn't a dry eye in the room. He said that for days afterward the men kept coming to him and telling him of little things that Mr. Warren had done for them. Some told how he'd followed them into a saloon and persuaded them to come out, how he'd stayed with them and walked out of his way night after night to go home with them and get them safely by temptation till they were strong enough to go alone. Some told how he'd stayed after hours and done their work when their wives or children were sick, and they needed to be away from the shop; and one man told how your father divided his pay with him for weeks when he was getting over an operation and could work only half-time. You are mistaken, Miss Warren; your father was a gentleman, and yours was a royal family if there ever was one. Do you know how Miss Cresson's father died? It was in a drunken row in some fine banquet-hall, and, before he died he had killed another man. Perhaps she is not so much to blame for being what she is with such a father, but tell me, which is the fine old family, yours or hers? I should prefer yours."

Chapter XIV

THE TEARS HAD COME now in spite of all Marion's struggles, though they were happy tears, and she tried to hurry them away with smiles.

"Oh," she said, "how beautiful of you, how beautiful to say that about my dear father! I knew he was all that and a great deal more, too, but I thought—I thought you would not count——"

"You thought that I was a snob," he said, smiling.

"Oh, no!" she said aghast. "Oh, no! I never thought that."

"Yes, yes, you did. There's no use in denying it. You thought, because I had enjoyed advantages that had not been yours that I would count those advantages greater than all other noble things in earth, and that I would despise you when I knew that you had been without them. Isn't that so?"

"No, not that exactly," she said with troubled look. "It was just that I thought you did not know, and that, when you found out, you would think I had not been honest with you to let you put yourself in that light before people. Isabel Cresson and all those girls know who I am. They probably thought it very strange of you to sit and talk with me when they were near by, and when they knew that I was such an insignificant little thing. It was not that I did not think you noble enough to be kind to me, even if you did know about me; but I was not one you would be likely to pick out for a friend, I knew, and I felt that I must make you understand it at once. It has troubled me all the week that I did not tell you last Saturday evening, but I did so want to go to-day—just this once more before——before——" she stopped in dismay, and knew not what to say.

"Before what?" he asked, watching her with gentle indulgence in his eyes.

"Why, before it ended," she finished bravely with scarlet cheeks.

"Then you thought I would drop you as soon as I knew?"

"Why, I supposed—that would be the end," she answered lamely.

"Answer me truly, and look right in my eyes," he insisted teasingly. "Did you really think I would drop you as soon as I knew? Please look up while you answer. You can't possibly deceive yourself into saying the wrong thing while you're looking at me, you know."

She raised her eyes in beautiful embarrassment to his, and wavered under his steady gaze.

"I thought—you—*ought* to."

"You thought I *ought?*" he laughed merrily. "Ah! Now, then, the question just once more; and please, if you don't mind, look up again for a minute. Did you *really* think I would drop you?"

"I——" there was a long pause, and then the eyes dropped in deep embarrassment—"I do not—know," she finished.

"Ah! Then you will admit just a little doubt of my criminality?" The troubled eyes gave him one beautiful look of reproach, and then the long lashes drooped on the crimson cheeks.

"Forgive me!" he said quickly. "I did not mean to tease you. I am sorry. I only wanted to be sure whether you thought me that kind of a fellow or not. Now let me assure you that I do not intend to drop you in the least. If there's any dropping, it will have to be done by you and not me. By the way, have you any idea where I first saw you?"

His ordinary tone reassured her, and she lifted her gaze once more shyly, the light coming into her eyes at the remembrance.

"Oh, yes, I shall never forget that, it was at the church. Mr. Radnor introduced you. I thought it so kind of him, because nobody else ever noticed me much. Mr. Radnor appreciated father a little, I think."

"He did, yes. I'm sure he did from some things he

said to me," said Lyman thoughtfully; then, frowning slightly at the memory of some other things Mr. Radnor had said; "but I don't think he appreciates his daughter as much as I do. He has never got well enough acquainted. Some day I hope he will."

Marion smiled.

"I don't suppose he'll ever see enough of me to know more than he does now about me. He is a very busy man, and I'm quite inconspicuous."

She spoke with a sweet humility, and the young man thought how very lovely she looked as she said it.

"Time changes all things," said Lyman, smiling. "You might find the order reversed, and Mr. Radnor may one day find you conspicuous enough on his horizon to warrant the time for appreciation. However, just at present I don't care much, do you? I prefer to appreciate you myself. And, by the way, you're all off about where I first saw you. I did not see you that night for the first time, by any means."

"Oh, you mean at the store when you brought the ribbon roses," she said. "Of course! How stupid of me! But I felt you did not recognize me then."

"Oh, but I did," he said; "but that wasn't the first time, either. I had seen you on several different occasions before that, besides once when I couldn't see you very well."

"Oh, what can you possibly mean?" she said, looking at him with such an air of utter bewilderment, as if her world had suddenly turned upside down, that he laughed joyfully again; and the deferential waiter, appearing just then to serve the first course, was relieved to see that his delay had not been noticed.

Marion sat wondering and watching while the waiter served them, laying so carefully before her the delicate china, heavy silver, and crystal as if she were a queen. How did it come that all this beauty and honor were for her even for a night? She could not understand it; and, looking up at the man across the table, she found her answer in his eyes, and her own drooped once more, while her heart beat rapid, joyous time in tune with the orchestra.

She dared not put into thoughts the thing she had seen in his eyes; yet it had entered her consciousness with a thrill that lifted the heavy weight she had been carrying all the week, and made her feel it was right to be happy in this good time, at least for to-night.

"Isn't it strange that there should be roses on the table just like mine to-night?" she said, suddenly laying her hand lovingly on the flowers at her breast.

The waiter was fussing with the silver covers of the soup-tureen which he had just brought; but he gave her a quick, knowing glance.

"Well, yes, that is a coincidence," said Lyman with a twinkle in his eye toward the solemn black man, who never stirred a muscle of his ebony countenance, though Lyman could see by the roll of his eyes that he was enjoying the little secret immensely. Then the soup was served, and the waiter betook himself to a suitable distance.

Now, Marion had eaten no lunch, and she had starved herself during the week as much as she dared for the sake of buying the new dress and hat, so that the delicious rich soup and the courses that followed were fully appreciated by her. But still the delightful new dishes kept appearing, and still the pleasant converse kept up its charm, until the girl dreaded the thought that the evening must soon be over, this great wonderful, beautiful evening in which there had been given to her a glimpse of the world of beauty she had never thought to enter.

"But what did you mean?" she dared shyly when they had finished a most delectable salad and were waiting for dessert. She had hoped her companion would answer this without her having to ask again; but, when the waiter left them, he had introduced another subject as if he delighted to leave it unanswered. "Where did you first see me?"

"At Harley's music-store, when you bought your first symphony tickets," he answered, watching her changing face delightedly.

Her eyes kindled with the happy memory.

"Oh! Were you there?"

"I was standing just behind you in the line, and heard you say you had never been before. I did a very bold thing, I'm afraid. I bought my ticket, and selected a seat as near the one you had chosen as possible, so that I might have the added delight of hearing a symphony in the vicinity of one who had never heard one before. Will you think I was very much to blame if I confess that I wanted to watch your face as you listened?"

"Oh!" said Marion with wonder in her eyes; and then she suddenly became terribly confused, and dropped her gaze from his. Why did this most unusual man say such strange things to her? Did he say them to other girls? Was it quite right to let him? Of course he meant nothing wrong by it; his face was too fine and pure to admit of a doubt about his having other than the noblest motives in all that he did; but did he quite understand how a girl felt when a man looked at her like that, and said such things? Perhaps girls who were used to society, and heard these nice things said to them every day, would not think anything about it; but she felt embarrassed, and did not know what to do. She lifted troubled eyes to his; and, seeing her embarrassment, he said in an easy tone:

"When are you going to tell me about your roses? I've been hoping for a long time that you would speak of them."

She was at her ease at once.

"Oh, would you care to know about them? Aren't they beautiful?' Aren't they *dear?* Almost like human faces! and such a deep, wonderful velvet! I've wanted to tell you about them two or three times; but I haven't had the courage, because, you see it's kind of a strange story, and you might not understand; for you see I don't know where they come from."

She touched the roses lightly, caressingly, with the tips of her fingers, and looked up to see what he would say.

"You don't know where they come from!"

She could not tell whether this was a question or an exclamation.

"No," she went on, "I don't know in the least. They come to me from time to time. I always think each time is the last, but to-day they came again."

"And you haven't the least suspicion who sends them?"

"No, not the least. At first I thought they were not sent to me at all, and it was all just a happening or mistake that I got them; but now the concerts are over, and these came to the store this morning, and there were lots of them. I was so glad. There were enough to wear all these and give one to each one of the girls in our

145

department. I liked having them to give even better than wearing them, and I had wished so much the last ones could have lived for me to wear to-day. Then, once before, some came to the house a day when I was not well enough to go to the store; and how could anyone know that? I don't understand it."

"Tell me about it. When did they begin to come?" His tone was low, and he was toying with his glass of water. He was not looking directly at her now. He seemed to be thinking hard.

"Why, I found the first one in my seat the night of the second symphony concert. I thought someone had dropped it, and laid it in the chair next to mine; but no one came to claim it. I asked an usher about it, but he only laughed and said that the owner probably had plenty more. But, when it happened again the next concert, I tried to find out who had left it there. I asked some women in the same gallery, but they acted as if I were impertinent to speak to them; so after that I kept the roses for myself, and they came every symphony night. I always found one there, all but the last night; and then there were two. I thought it was a kind of good-by, and I kept them in water until every leaf fell. I couldn't bear to put them away in the box with the rest of the dead ones. I made them last as long as possible. And then these came to-day just when I wanted them."

"Who do you think sent them?" His tone was still quiet, and his gaze downward.

"I don't know at all," she said. "At first I tried to think of someone I could see who might have done it. Down in the balcony where we went to-day there was a beautiful old lady with a silvery dress and lovely white hair. I pleased myself by thinking maybe someone like that had sent them because she saw I was a girl alone, and perhaps she thought I looked like someone she had loved, or something. Then it came to me that perhaps someone had my seat last year who had a friend who used to send roses and didn't know she was gone away, and so the roses kept coming; but that wouldn't explain those that came to the house and the store; and so I didn't know what to think, and I just thought God knew I needed them, and so He sent them; and I thanked Him, for I hadn't anyone else to thank."

146

Her voice had grown low and sweet, and the eyes across the table looked at her with reverence, and, when she looked up, his tenderness almost blinded her. It seemed so very much what she needed, and yet couldn't expect to have, of course.

"I have something to tell you," he said very gently and with a voice full of feeling. "Suppose we take a walk. Do you like to walk? Do you feel like walking? Or would you prefer to stay here awhile?"

"I love to walk," said Marion with delight. "I haven't had a good walk for a long, long time. Father and I used to go when he had a Saturday afternoon off, or sometimes when he came home early in the evenings and wasn't too tired."

"Then let us walk," said Lyman with satisfaction, rising from his chair. "The moon is almost full, and the Avenue will not be crowded by this time. There will be opportunity to talk."

"It will be beautiful," said the girl wistfully; "but I have already taken a great deal of your day."

"I shall be only too pleased to give you the rest of it," he said, smiling, "and as many more as you will take."

Then he turned to the waiter, and said in a low tone, "Just put this on my account."

It was a common enough sentence, but it startled Marion.

"Put this on my account!" Then this man was accustomed to come to this wonderful place and partake of such repasts! Nothing that he could have said would have so impressed the girl who listened with a sense of the difference between his station and hers. And a man like this had been giving her his time and attention!

Doubtless it was but a passing whim. Very likely he brought other girls to this beautiful place after other concerts. She was to him but a psychological study; and, when he had conned her little life awhile, and analyzed and tabulated her species, she would soon be forgotten. But need she resent that? Might she not take this pleasant spot in life, knowing it was fleeting, and enjoy it while it lasted? Would it leave a pain greater than the pleasure when it was gone, because of what she missed? Well, she must look well to herself that she did not let the joy enter into her soul too deep. It was to be like her roses, fleeting but sweet.

With this thought passing through her mind she walked the length of the palm-girded rooms and out into the lovely night.

It was lovely even in the city, for the moon was nearly full, and the air was balmy with the promise of spring, yet held a tang of bracing air left over from the winter to give a zest to the walk.

Lyman led her quickly through the more crowded part of the streets and out to the Avenue, where pedestrians were not too many for comfort, and where the fine pavement and the brilliant lighting made a beautiful place for a promenade.

He had drawn her hand firmly within his arm when they started, and dropped his step into unison with her own; and she could not but feel the exhilaration of walking so.

"Now!" said he when they were come into the broad part of the Avenue, where they did not have to thread their way so carefully between people, and it was quieter for talking. "Now would you like *me* to tell *you* about your roses?"

"Oh, do *you* know where they came from? Do you know who sent them?"

He felt her hand trembling on his arm, and her eyes looked anxiously into his. She knew the time of revelation had come, and she dreaded to hear about them, lest it would make them less her own. With tenderness he laid his own hand over hers, and kept it there. Looking down into her eyes, he said in a low tone:

"Don't you know now? Can't you guess who it was?"

She searched his face, and hesitated, then read his answer there.

"Oh, it was not—it could not have been—it—*was—you!*"

There were awe, and delight, and then real alarm in her voice, as her conviction became a certainty, and she began to realize what it all meant.

He was troubled at her silence.

"Are you glad or sorry it was I?" he asked anxiously.

She did not answer for a moment; and then, looking down with troubled air, she said half tremblingly,

"Oh, why—why—did—you—do—it?"

He felt the moment had come, and he was not half so sure of her as he had been a little while before.

"Because I loved you from the first minute I saw you, and I wanted to win you for my wife," he answered in a low, intense voice.

Chapter XV

"FOR YOUR WIFE!" she repeated in wonder, as if she had not heard aright. "You would not choose *me* for your *wife!*"

"I surely do," he said tenderly, "I want it more than I ever wanted anything in my life before. I tell you I have loved you ever since that first morning. I could not get the vision of your fresh, sweet face out of my mind. It stayed with me all day long, and I looked for you eagerly at the first concert."

"How wonderful!" answered Marion in a low, sweet voice as if she had just received a message from a heavenly visitant and angel wings were still visible to her eye.

"Didn't the roses tell you that someone loved you?"

"They tried to, but I wouldn't let them."

"Why wouldn't you let them?"

"Because I was afraid. I didn't see how it could ever come true. I was sure no one for whom I could care would ever care for me."

"And, now that you know, do you think you could care for me?" He asked the question tenderly, looking down into her face as they walked slowly down the bright avenue, utterly oblivious of the other pedestrians.

She lifted her eyes to him wonderingly.

"How could I help it?" she asked. "I've cared from the first minute you spoke to me, and I have been so troubled about it I did not know what to do. I almost decided to go to Vermont and live with my brother, and get away from temptation. It seemed so terrible in me to dare to care for you, *you!* Oh, I don't see how I'm ever to believe it. And I don't think it can be right for me to accept this great thing. I'm sure you don't understand how ignorant and untrained I am."

"My darling!" said he. "Don't! I cannot bear to hear you say those things about yourself. I love you for yourself and not for your attainments. Those things are only outside matters. We will study together, you and I."

"Oh!" breathed the girl, "I could not think of anything more beautiful in life than that——"

"You darling!" he said again. "If you keep on looking at me like that, I shall be obliged to kiss you right here on the street; and that would be scandalous, I suppose."

"Oh!" gasped Marion, dropping her eyes in alarm, while the lovely waves of color rushed into her cheeks.

"There! Don't be frightened," he laughed. "I'll remember the conventionalities; only you really make it very hard work when you put on that adorable look. Tell me, did you like the roses?"

"Like them! I—*loved* them. But how did you do it? It is so wonderful! It is all wonderful."

"Oh, it was easily managed. I just went early, and got in as soon as the doors were open. In fact, I bribed one of the doorkeepers to let me in early, and then put the rose in your chair, and went down to the proscenium box to watch for you. You almost caught me once when you came so early. I was just going up the last step at the left-hand door when you entered the middle door. I waited to watch you through the crack that time. And do you remember when you asked the usher what to do with your first rose? I was standing boldly in the doorway, talking to the other usher all the time. I wanted to be sure that you took my rosebud home with you."

"Oh!" said Marion. It seemed to be her one available word.

"Do you remember a night when it rained, and you went home in the car? Did you know I walked home with you from the corner, and held my umbrella over you? I doubt if you realized it, for you must have got just as wet as if you had been alone, it was blowing so hard."

"Oh, was it you?" Her eyes glowed at him again. "I called a 'Thank you' into the darkness. Did you hear me? I always thought I heard an answer."

"I answered you," he said eagerly. "I said, 'You're welcome, dear.' To be sure, I whispered the 'dear' to myself; but didn't your heart hear it, dear?"

"I believe it did," she answered softly; "only I didn't know what made me so happy. I thought it was the rose."

They walked on fully absorbed in each other, the blocks counting into one, two, three miles.

"And did you know from the first that I worked in the store?" she asked once.

"No, I had to ferret that out. After that night in the rain, when I found out where you lived, I was determined to make a way to be introduced. I made errands down that way day after day, changing the hour, and walking up and down the street, or riding past, hoping to catch a glimpse of you. At last it occurred to me that, coming from that neighborhood and a plain house, you very likely had to earn your living. Your interest in the concerts made me think of music naturally, but careful listening could never even imagine a sound of music coming from your abiding-place. I felt sure you could not be a music teacher or there would have been a piano heard sometimes. I thought perhaps you taught school——"

"That was what father wanted for me," she interrupted sadly.

"So I went very early to the street, but not early enough to catch you yet. Then I thought of stenography and bookkeeping."

"All too high for me to attempt," she murmured humbly.

"At last, about a week after I began to watch I went one morning before it was quite daylight, and tramped up and down, always in sight of the house, until I was rewarded by seeing you come out. You haven't any idea how my heart pounded as I turned to follow you at a discreet distance. I never felt so shy in my life. I met a policeman a few blocks on the way, and he looked at me half suspiciously, I thought, as if I must appear guilty. But you walked calmly on, and never seemed to notice that your steps were being followed."

"Oh, how frightened I should have been if I had known!" she exclaimed.

"Am I so formidable?"

Then they both laughed and began again.

"I saw you enter the door for employees, and then I

had a long search through the departments until I found you. I began at last to despair, and to suspect that you were hidden away in some mysterious work-room on a top floor, or in some dull office; but I finally came upon you, all by chance, right in the midst of the beautiful colors of all those ribbons. That day I celebrated by having you make me some roses. Have you forgotten?"

"Forgotten! How could I? I've often wondered about them. I thought then they were for your wife. The girls all said so. They said your wife must be very happy to have you care so much for her."

"I hope she will be happy," he said reverently. "I shall make it my business to do all I can in that direction. Yes, I guess the roses were for my wife, though I wanted them for myself till she came to me. I will give them to you, my wife, on our wedding morning. How soon can that be?"

"Oh!" said Marion softly, "Oh!" and then, "Oh, I don't know." Her eyes drooped, and her whole countenance took on a troubled look.

"Couldn't we be married right away?" he asked. "Is there anything or anybody to hinder? I haven't told you a bit about myself yet, have I? Perhaps you won't feel like trusting me until you've known me longer, though."

"Oh, it isn't that!" said the girl quickly. "It never could be that. It's only that I—that there are so many things—so much for me to do first before I could be fit—ready—ever to marry you—if I ever really could be."

"What things? Clothes, do you mean?"

"Yes, clothes, and other things, and I'd have a great deal to learn. I don't know that I could ever learn it all."

"And why should you? I thought we were going to study together. What right would you have to go off and study things by yourself? And, as for the clothes, I always thought that was the silliest of all silly reasons to keep a man away from his wife for weeks and weeks after they have found out they love each other and decided to get married. I don't want a lot of fine clothes for a wife, I want you, now, just as you are. You're sweet enough and pretty enough and fine enough to please me always; and, if you need a lot of new things, it shall be my pride and pleasure to buy them for you. You'll have plenty of time to select what you want, and can go about it in a leisurely way. I can assure you I'm not going to be a bit patient about this. I want you right away. Couldn't you arrange to marry me some day next week? I've got to go up to Boston on a business trip, and I want to take you with me. I can't bear to go and leave you——"

"Oh, no!" gasped Marion. "I couldn't possibly. Oh! Why, you've only just told me about it——"

"Dear," said he tenderly pressing the hand he held, "I'm not going to frighten you with my haste; and we'll do things decently and in order as you wish it, of course; but you forget that I've been thinking of this all winter; and perhaps you don't know it, but I'm a very lonesome man. I need you tremendously. I've nobody to love me and nobody to love except the world at large. Mother died two years ago. She had been an invalid for ten years, and she and I had travelled together a great deal whenever she was able. I have missed her more than I can tell you, since she went away. I live in a great big house, with two old servants who have been with us since I was a boy. They do their best to make it comfortable, but they cannot make a home and I want you there with your brightness and beauty. I want to be with you and have your companionship in my work and pleasure. Must I wait? Couldn't you make it next week? Are you afraid of me? Don't you love me enough to come to me right away?"

As he told of his mother, her other hand had stolen up and touched his gently, as if she wanted to console him for his loss; and he gathered it with the other in his clasp.

"I love you enough to come right away, of course," she said; and her voice was clear and steady now. "It isn't that; it's only that I feel so unready in mind and ways; and then, I've really no things such as other people get married in. I shouldn't feel right not to get *some* things ready; and then, besides, there's the store. You know when we sign the contract we promise to give a month's notice if we are going to leave. It wouldn't be fair to them."

"Don't worry about the store," he said joyously. "Chapman's a good friend of mine. It would need only a word from me to get you off in a hurry. I'll see to that if you'll give me permission. I want you. I need you; why, I—*love* you, dear! Can't you see? You wouldn't let clothes and things stand in the way of that, would you?"

In the end he had his way. When did a man not have his way who talked like that? Marion had the feeling that she had suddenly been invited to enter heaven all as she was, arrayed in earthly garments; nevertheless a great joy and sweetness came down upon her. She could scarcely realize her own gladness, it was so great. She had not yet got used to knowing that he loved her and that he had been the giver of the roses that had gladdened her heart all winter; and here was this great question of marriage pushed in, for which she felt so unfit.

"I'm not at all the kind of wife you ought to have," she said faintly after her last protest had been silenced. "People will pity you, and think you have demeaned yourself to marry a lowly person. Isabel will think——"

"Never mind what Isabel thinks. I'll warrant you one thing, she will be among the first to call upon my wife."

"And oh, what shall I do? How shall I act?" Marion almost stopped in her walk, aghast at the prospect.

"You'll act just your own sweet natural self, dear," he said; "and she will go away and say how very charming you are, and how she has known you and admired you all her life. Oh, don't I know her? She is a cunning one, and she will not leave you off her calling-list. There are reasons why she will prefer to pose as your intimate friend. As for other people, I'm not afraid that my wife will not win her sweet way wherever she goes; and, if any dare to think in my presence any such thing as you have mentioned, I shall be glad to teach them otherwise. Now, dear, you are not to think this thing about yourself another minute. You are yourself, and just what I want. You are the only woman in the whole world that I love and want for my wife. Besides that, you're tired; for we've walked miles, and now we're going home in a taxi; and you're going to rest to-night, and to-morrow afternoon you're going to let me come and take you out in my car, where we shall be alone and can talk together. Then perhaps in the evening we'll go to church together, and horrify dear Isabel just once more before she finds she has to change her tactics."

An hour later in her room Marion stood before her mirror and surveyed herself critically. The new dress was undeniably pretty and the new hat becoming; roses and cheeks vied with each other in glowing crimson; and her eyes had not lost their starry look. But she was not admiring herself as she stood and looked earnestly. She was looking into the soul of this self that smiled back to her, and searching it to see whether she could find the old self anywhere, and whether it were really Marion Warren, the little ribbon-girl who had lived her lonely life for a whole year, struggling upward toward the great things she had longed for. And was this life suddenly to be all changed, and she to be put down in the midst of the larger life, where she was to be not an insignificant learner merely, but a most important part in a truly great man's life? Could it be true? Wasn't she dreaming?

Then the searching went deeper, and she looked into the eyes in the glass to see whether she could find any trace of the woman that was to be, out of the self that she was. Was it possible for her to fulfil the great ideal of the man who had chosen her out of all the world to be his wife? Then her great love answered for her, and she smiled back an assurance to the girl in the glass who questioned.

"I will do my best; and, if he is satisfied, nothing else matters," she murmured softly to herself.

Then she turned to look about on her little room with new eyes. There it all was just as she had left it in the early morning, everything in order, only her scissors and some bits of silk scraps on the desk betraying her last bit of preparation for this wonderful afternoon. There was the small box of provisions standing by the partly open window, from which she had expected to get her meagre supper after the concert should be over. To think now how superfluous any supper seemed after that wonderful dinner!

As she looked about her room, it seemed but half familiar, as if it had been weeks instead of hours since she left it. Could it be that it was but this morning that she had gone out from here expecting to return at night with the burden of a closed friendship on her heart? And now here she stood, the promised wife of the man she loved, and a whole story of revelation wrapped up in the crimson buds at her breast to be read and reread at her leisure; and all the to-morrows of more beautiful pages still to be written for her in the future!

There came slow steps up the stairs, and the tired voice of the landlady called out:

"Here's a letter fer ye, Miss Warren. The postman brung it this mornin', an' I thought you might like it right off; so I come up. It was layin' on the hall table, but I guess you didn't take notice to it when you come along by."

"Oh, thank you, Mrs. Nash. That's very kind," she said. "No, I didn't notice any letter for me. I wasn't expecting one to-night."

Her radiant face and happy voice attracted the tired woman.

"You're lookin' most awful pretty to-night," she said, lingering. "Them roses is like some my grandmother used to raise on a little bush by her kitchen window. I ain't see none exactly that color since I was a girl, till you sent me down them that day. My! but that's a nice hat, and you look real good in it."

She surveyed the girl admiringly.

The old woman came into the room, and dropped into the nearest chair, wrapping her hands in her checked apron, as if she had something on her mind. "I been noticing them roses you get so often," she began again. "Some man'll be tryin' to carry you off purty soon. I've seen it comin'. No such pretty, sweet girl as you would stay long by herself lonesomelike. It ain't accordin' to nature, an' I s'pose it's all right; but it's a turrible lottery, marriage is. I hope the man you've been keepin' comp'ny with ain't got no bad habits. If he should turn out to drink, don't have him, Miss Warren, no matter how fair he speaks. It's no use trustin' 'em; the poor things can't help it when once drink gets at 'em. I hope he makes a good livin', an' you won't have to work no more. I hope you'll turn out to get a good man, my dear. You certainly deserve it more 'n most."

Marion's cheeks flamed scarlet but she answered smilingly, "You needn't worry about me, Mrs. Nash. He's all right, and I shall not have to work any more."

"Well, my dear, I s'pose you'd think so anyway, whatsomever he was. But I hope your belief comes true, I do. You've been a good lodger, and I'll not get another as good in many a long day; I am sure of that."

When the old woman had toiled downstairs again, Marion opened her letter.

Chapter XVI

THE LETTER SEEMED remote from her, as if it were
written to her in a former state of existence and had no
relation to her present circumstances. She knew it was
Tom's writing. Jennie had written occasionally since they
went away; but usually it was to ask about fashions or
request her sister-in-law to make some purchases for her,
with always a sharp dig at the end of the letter because
Marion chose to stay in the city. The girl felt almost too
happy to-night to be interested in a letter from anywhere;
but, as she read, her face softened, and tears gathered in
her eyes.

Dear Marion: (it read) I've made up my mind to write and
tell you that we think it is about time you quit this business
of staying in the city alone, and come up to live with us.
Father wouldn't like you to be off like that. My conscience
has troubled me ever since we went away. I think I ought to
have stayed in the city another year for your sake, and given
you a little more schooling if you wanted it so much. I thought
you'd soon see how foolish it was, and come to us; but you've
got pluck. I always knew that; and I ought to have seen you'd
get what you wanted. I never could understand why you
wanted it; but, seeing you did, you ought to have had it. Now
I've got a proposition to make. You come home this summer, and help with the housework, especially during harvest,
and help Jennie sew things up, and teach the children a little;
and then, if you don't like it up here, we'll all go down to the
village to live. There's a real good normal school there; and
you can study winters if you want to, and be home summers.
There's another thing, too. I've felt mean about the money
for that house. It was half yours, you know, and you had a
right to it. Father always said he'd made a will, and I can't

158

help thinking by what he said at the last that he meant to leave the house to you. Anyhow half of it was yours and I oughtn't to have taken it. Of course it's all in the house now, and I can't very well get it out for four or five years yet; but I'll pay you interest on your part, and, if you don't want to live here, you shall have your share, if I'm prospered, as soon as I can conveniently take it out. I'm sending you a check for a hundred and fifty dollars. Things went pretty well with us, better than I expected for a first year; and I can spare this just as well as not. Get yourself anything you need and live comfortably; but I hope you'll decide to accept my proposition and come home for the summer anyway. Then we'll try to fix things to suit somehow. Jennie says she wishes you'd come, too. I don't like to think of my little sister all alone in a big city. It isn't the thing in these days when so many things happen. Of course I don't want to hinder you in what you want to do, but I think you better decide to come home.

Your affectionate brother,

Tom.

It was the longest letter Tom had ever written, and it warmed his sister's heart to have it come now in the midst of her other joy, that she might feel that her own were loving toward her also.

She was glad to the depths of her soul that she did not have to accept his proposition and go to that home to live. But he had asked her in a humble, loving way and sent that generous check.

She would be able now to buy a number of necessities and a few luxuries to replenish her meagre wardrobe. For it hurt her pride terribly to think of going to her husband like a shabby little beggar girl. And the savings from her tiny salary were so very small that she knew she could get very few, even simple wedding garments with it.

Also, there was another reason why she was glad of that letter. It made it seem reasonably sure that Tom never knew about the will, else he would not have written as he had. She rejoiced that she might once more have faith in her brother.

When she lay down to sleep, it was with a great joy in her heart. She felt again the thrill of Lyman's hand upon hers; his voice when he first said, "I love you"; his lips upon hers in good-night.

He came the next afternoon, and the gloomy little parlor

wore its most dustless front, with three crayon portraits of landlady Nash's deceased husband, son, and daughter respectively, smiling down upon it all.

Mrs. Nash herself, with most unexpected fineness of soul, sent in, when they returned from their ride, a tray containing hot biscuits, pressed chicken, honey, two cups of tea, and a plate of sugar cookies. She had said to herself:

"What if me own daughter had lived, an' been alone in a strange boardin'-house!"—and this had been the result.

The pretty new hat and the dress went to church that evening with two quiet roses nestling among its folds. Miss Cresson, seated across the aisle, spent the hour of service in thoughtful meditation; and the theme of her cogitations was, "Is *that* who she was?"

"How long have you gone to this church?" asked Marion of Lyman as they were on their way home. "I don't remember having seen you before that reception."

"My grandfather was one of the founders of that church," he said. "I've always gone there when I was at home. But I've been away a good many years altogether, counting school and college, and war, and travel afterward. I sighted you the first thing when I got back, however. You must have been a very small girl when I went away."

"It is all just a fairy dream," said the girl joyfully. "How could it ever have happened to me?"

"Because you are the princess," said Lyman, smiling.

The fairy story continued to unfold the next morning. Just a little before her lunch-hour she was sent for to come to the office, where she was told that her services had been most valuable to the firm, and that, while deep regret was felt at the thought of losing her, she was at liberty to leave them immediately if she felt it imperative. They would, however, take it as a great favor if she would remain for two or three days to instruct a substitute. Also she was handed a generous check which she was told was the office's appreciation of the unique work in the store. Mr. Chapman said some very pleasant things, which brought the rosy flush to her cheeks; and the tone in which he spoke of Lyman made her heart throb with pride. The deference with which he treated her was a marked contrast to his brief, abrupt manner of their first interview.

She knew that Lyman had been to Mr. Chapman as he had promised to do the night before. It was beautiful to her that he had cast the mantle of his own personality about her.

With the pleasant, kindly wishes of the official head of the firm ringing in her ears Marion went from the office to meet Lyman, as had been agreed upon.

They took lunch in a quiet little restaurant this time, where a sheltered table at the end of the room gave them opportunity for conversation.

After the order had been given Lyman took from his pocket a tiny white leather box, and handed it to the wondering girl.

She opened it shyly, not guessing what it contained.

Inside was a crimson velvet case with a white pearl spring. The crimson of the velvet was the same shade as the rose she wore. Had he matched it on purpose? Still wondering, she took out the case and touched the spring. There against its white velvet lining flashed a glorious diamond.

She caught her breath, and looked at him, almost frightened by the magnificence of it.

"Put it on," he said. "It may not fit, and then I'll have to have it changed. I stole your glove last night when you dropped it on the floor as we said good-night. I had to get the measurement from that."

"Is it for me?" she asked with such an illumination of her whole face that he was almost awed by the effect of his gift.

"Surely! Who else could it be for? Put it on quick, before the waitress comes. Here, hide the box"; and he reached out, and took possession of the box and case in time to prevent the waitress from enjoying a bit of delightful gossip with her fellow laborers.

The ring fitted perfectly, and after the waitress had left them alone once more the little hand with its unusual adornment stole out to the edge of the table, and revealed itself; but, when Marion lifted her eyes, they were glittering with unshed tears.

"What is it, dear?" he asked anxiously. "Have I hurt you in any way? Don't you like it?"

"Oh, it is wonderful, wonderful!" she said, "and I was thinking how pleased Father would be to have you care for me like that."

"Dear little girl!" said the man, reverently leaning toward her and speaking in a low voice. "That is only a small symbol of how much I love you. I hope to make my life tell you plainer than that."

She gave him a smile of radiant brightness.

The precious lunch-hour was soon over, and she felt that she must hasten back to the store. As they rose to go out, he said:

"I want you to promise me one thing. Don't get a lot of clothes, please. Just fix up what you want for the wedding, and let's buy anything else you need in New York. It will be delightful to go shopping with you, and help you pick out things, if you don't mind having me around."

He was rewarded with another brilliant smile of reassurance.

"It will be beautiful, inexpressibly so, to have you always around," she said with shining eyes.

She went back to her ribbons as quietly that afternoon as if nothing wonderful had happened; but there was a light in her eyes and a glow on her cheeks that were presently detected by her co-laborers; and it was not many minutes before they had discovered the flashing of the beautiful diamond on her finger. It was whispered from one to another, till finally the boldest of them all laughingly challenged her to tell where it came from. She smiled shyly over the rosette she was making, and acknowledged that she was engaged; and they kissed her and congratulated her, and said they hoped she would not leave them soon.

Their kindness was very pleasant. They had not all seemed to be so very friendly heretofore, except when they wanted a favor; but it was pleasant to have them nice to her, even though she did recognize that her roses and her diamond had paved the way for their effusiveness.

Late that afternoon, when customers were growing less and the new girl she was teaching did not need help for a few minutes, she stole away for a little while, and reconnoitred for the purchases she must make.

It was almost closing-time when Lyman came down the aisle, and stopped before her counter.

162

"I may walk home with you, may I not?" he asked in a low tone, his eyes answering her glad look in greeting. "Where shall I meet you?"

"Why, I can go with you now in just a minute. I've closed up my book and sent it in. Wait by the door at the end of the aisle while I run up to the coatroom for my things."

He watched her as she rapidly and skilfully rolled the ends of two or three bolts of ribbon smoothly, and pinned them in place, putting them on the shelf, and touching them gently as if she loved their rosy tints and silken texture, the ring flashing on her white hand caressingly.

She turned brightly to the other girls, who were huddled together at the upper end of the counter, watching and whispering softly about her.

"Good-night, girls; it's my turn to go early to-night."

"Good-night!" they chorused eagerly as if they wished to show their good will before her friend.

They watched Marion and Lyman walk together down the aisle.

"She's in luck!" remarked one girl. "He's one of the swellest of the swells. He's no snob, either. He's the real thing. Did you take notice to that diamond, girls? Wasn't it a peach? He's some classy bridegroom, all right."

"Well, she deserves it!" unexpectedly snapped a sharp-faced elderly saleswoman whose plain face and plainer speech were not relished by the girls, and who seldom had a pleasant word for anyone.

"She certainly does," agreed the rest. "If anybody can have good times and not be spoiled by them, she can. She's an angel if there ever was one, and she'll never be too proud to speak to her old friends, I'll bet."

"I don't believe she will," said another. "Gee! Wasn't that a diamond, though? I'd like to get on to a job like that myself, but they aren't just lying around loose."

"If they were, you'd never get one, Fan. It wouldn't go with all those glass rings and bracelets you've got on!"

The girl in question looked down on her cheap jewelry, contemplatively chewing her gum.

"Well, I s'pose I wouldn't fit," she said; "but I'm real glad she's got him, anyway. It makes you feel kind of good inside to have things like that happen once in a while. There goes the bugle. Good-night, girls; I'm booked

163

for a moving-picture show to-night. Billy asked me, and I s'pose Billy's good enough for me. Anyhow, I like him. Good-night."

The next two days went like a sweet dream. Marion had fully made up her mind what she needed for her wedding-day and the journey, and with her two checks she found it quite possible to get these things of the best. The gown she had set her heart upon in her dreams for several weeks was still in a glass case up in the French department. It was a simple affair of dark-blue cloth with lines that only imported things from great artists seem able to achieve, and she knew it was to be marked down on account of the approach of spring. Her discount as an employee would bring it down still lower and put it quite within her means; and she knew its distinguished simplicity would give her the quiet, suitable appearance that Lyman's wife should have. A black hat from the French room went well with this.

A becoming little dinner gown of georgette, some fine, well-chosen lingerie and a few other dainty accessories completed her modest outfit. She had promised not to get much, but what she got should be of the best, and worthy of the position she was to occupy as the wife of a man of wealth and influence.

She had as yet no adequate idea of how wealthy or influential Lyman was. He dressed quietly, and he never spoke of his circumstances. Indeed, she thought little about it herself except to feel her own unworthiness.

One fact, however, served to open her eyes somewhat. On Tuesday evening, when she reached her lodging-place, she found two large packages that had arrived during the day, addressed to herself. She opened them eagerly, and found that one contained a set of beautiful heavy silver spoons of the latest pattern, engraved with her own initials and bearing the personal card of Mr. Chapman. The other when unwrapped proved to be a massive bowl of solid silver, costly and magnificent, and bearing the congratulations of the firm.

She had heard stories of the fine wedding-gifts that had been given to employees in the past, but nothing to equal these; and she had sense enough to see that for her own sake such costly gifts would never have been hers. These did more than anything else to fill her with awe and almost dread for her new position, and to make her feel the wide gulf, social and financial, which existed between herself and the man who had chosen her for his wife.

She placed the glittering array of silver on her little white bed, and sat down on the floor before it. Then suddenly her head bowed beside it. How could she ever live up to those elegant wedding-gifts? Oh, it was all a mistake, a dreadful mistake. She was just a plain little, common girl, and she never could be a rich man's wife.

Then in the midst of her agitation the maid of all work brought up Lyman's card with three great crimson roses; and she hurried down to him, all fearful as she was.

He heard her protest, and, gathering her in his arms, laid his lips upon hers in token of his love for her and his strength that should be hers to overcome all such difficulties and differences.

"But won't you be sorry by and by when you know me better and see the difference?" she asked, fearful even yet.

"Will you?" he asked. "Dear, there's just as much difference between you and me as there is between me and you. Did you never think of that? If there's anything to feel, you'll feel it just as much as I."

"No," said Marion, shaking her head; "I'm sure you feel it *down* more than you feel it *up*."

"It looks to me as though you were trying to feel it 'up,' as you call it, more than I do what you are pleased to say is 'down,' though that, dear, remember, I deny. You are not down. In real things I know you are far ahead of me. You have much to teach me, dear, of faith in God. What difference does the rest make? It was nice of the firm to send us that. I've known them all always, and they were friends of father's. Chapman is a good friend also. He would of course send you something nice. There'll be a lot more things when people find it out. I'll be interested to see what Miss Cresson will send. If it were in the days of the ancients, it might perhaps be a serpent ring with eyes of rubies and a secret spring concealing a drop of poison; but I scarcely think in these days there'll be danger of that. She'll probably content herself with a silver pheasant or a pair of andirons. Come on, let's sit down and talk business."

Chapter XVII

THE NEXT MORNING MARION told the girls that it was her last day with them, and many were the outcries of dismay. They could not get over it, and hovered about her between customers, until people looked curiously and wondered why that extremely pretty girl in the plain black dress wore so gorgeous a diamond, and how she made her hair wave so beautifully. Before night the news of her marriage on the morrow had spread among all her acquaintances in the store, and they kept coming one by one to wish her well and leave with her some gift or remembrance, until the shelves around her were overflowing with packages little and big, and she had to send a lot of them up to the cloak-room to make room for the ribbons.

It seemed that Marion had more friends than she had known.

There was the pale little girl who carried up the ribbon bows to the millinery department on the eighth floor. She brought Marion a lovely fine handkerchief, with hand embroidery. Marion had taken ten minutes of her lunch-hour once to run up in her place when the girl had a headache.

There was the sharp-faced maiden lady who made things unpleasant for the others at the ribbon-counter. Her gift was a collar and cuffs of real lace.

The girl who chewed gum and wore glass rings presented her with a handsome silk umbrella with a silver handle of the latest model. She knew a good thing when she saw it if she did prefer "Billy."

The floor-walker in her vicinity brought a bronze clock; the head man of the department offered a silver-link handbag; and one little errand boy, whom Marion had kindly

166

helped out of several scrapes brought on by his love of fun, brought her a gold thimble.

There were handkerchiefs and scarfs and pins and bracelets, jardinières and candlesticks, and lamps, a book or two, and three pictures, not always well chosen, but all bringing to her a revelation of good will and kindly fellowship that made her heart leap with joy. These with whom she had been working during the past year were all her friends. How nice it would have been if she could have understood it all along!

It was being whispered about that she was to marry some one of high degree in social circles, and all of them showed her that they were proud of her for having done so well. There did not seem to be one among them all who felt jealous or hard toward her for having the opportunity to pass into an easier life than theirs. Even the old janitor, who had every day cleared away the rubbish from the spent ribbon bolts, came with his offering, a little brown bulb in a pretty clear glass of pebbles and water. He told her it would bloom some day for her just as her pretty face had bloomed for them in the store, God bless her.

And Marion put her hand into his rough one and thanked him as she might have thanked her own dear father.

But the day was over at last, and weary and happy, Marion went back to her little top floor room for the last night.

Lyman had promised to come for her at half past eight, and long before he arrived she was ready with her modest outfit packed in her handsome new suitcase, and looking as pretty as a bride could wish to look.

Mrs. Nash had sent up a nice breakfast; but Marion was too excited to eat much, though she tried to do so to please the old landlady. Most of the time she spent quietly kneeling beside her white bed, praying to be made fit for the place she was going to try to fill in the world, and thanking her heavenly Father.

With the blessings of her landlady ringing loudly in her ears Marion stepped from the door to behold a handsome limousine waiting at the curbstone. The small children of the street were drawn up in frank amazement to stare. The dark, quiet elegance of the car, its silver mountings and inconspicuous monogram, proclaimed its patrician ownership. A chauffeur in livery stood awaiting orders.

The girl hesitated on the door-step. Was she to ride in that great, beautiful car to her wedding? A sudden fearful shyness took possession of her. Lyman helped her into the tonneau, and with a word to the chauffeur took his place beside her. The seat in front of them held a great sheaf of white roses, and beyond the roses loomed the immaculate back of the chauffeur.

She felt out of place amid all this elegance. The newness of her own attire made her feel still more strange. Would she ever be at home in this new world that she was about to enter? Perhaps she had been wrong to accept; perhaps he would be sorry. Oh, perhaps——

Then quietly a hand was laid upon hers.

"Darling," he said in a low tone, "don't be frightened! See, the roses. They are white for my bride, but I had one great red one hidden underneath them all. Look!" He reached over with his free hand, and lifted the upper rows of heavy white buds; and there, nestling in the hidden green, lay one great deep, dark crimson bud.

The sight of it reassured the girl. With a rush of gladness she turned to him.

"Oh, you are so good to me!" she cried. "Won't you ever be sorry it was only I? Won't you ever wish it was somebody wiser and better?"

"Never, darling!" he said, and the look in his eyes reassured her more than his words could have done.

Then in a moment it seemed they were at the church.

One white bud broke off, as they were taking the flowers from the car, and Marion gave it to a little lame child who was leaning on her crutch to watch them. She smiled on the child, and the little girl answered with such a ravishing smile of thanks that Marion felt it was a kind of benediction.

There were beautiful lights in the empty church from the great stained-glass windows. The spring sunshine lit up the face of the Christ in the window behind the pulpit. There were ferns and palms and white and crimson roses, a few of them about the platform; and the minister stood gravely, smiling with his eyes. The organ was play-

ing, too, softly, as they came in, yet with a note of tr
in the sweet old wedding-march.

Marion, coming shyly up the aisle, her hand resting ʌn
the arm of the man she loved, was filled with wonder
and awe over it all. Who trimmed the church with roses
for her? How did it happen that the organist was there
for her quiet little wedding? Oh, it was all his love, his
great, wonderful love about her. It was a miracle of love
for her. Could she ever be worthy of it all?

As she turned from the minister's final words and bless-
ing, she felt that the wedding-ceremony was the most
beautiful she had ever heard. Every word seemed written
in her heart, and with her whole soul she echoed the
vows she had made.

The minister's wife blessed her lovingly and Marion
felt as if she were not so friendless after all.

A moment more, and they were back in the car and
speeding away. Marion did not question whither until
they stopped once more, and she looked up in surprise.

"We're going to have our wedding-breakfast now,
dear," said Lyman. "I was hoping you would not eat
anything before you left the house. Did you? Come, confess!"

He led her laughing into a small, lovely room where a
round table was set for two; and here, too, the table was
smothered in red and white roses and asparagus ferns.
From a quick glance as they entered she recognized it as
the most exclusive hotel in the city, and again her foolish
fears came down upon her. She was fairly afraid of the
silent servants who did everything with such machine-like
perfection. She found her only safety in keeping her eyes
on her husband's face and realizing that he was master of
the situation, and she belonged to him; therefore she need
not fear. He would see that she did not do anything out
of the way.

After they had been served, and were about to go away,
Marion looked at the roses lovingly, and bent her face
down to the table.

"You dear things! I'm sorry to leave you behind, though
I've so many more," she said, smiling. Then, looking at
Lyman: "How I wish the girls at the ribbon-counter could
have a glimpse of them! They would think this table so
wonderful."

A good idea!" said Lyman. "It isn't far from here. Symonds," turning to the head waiter, "can you leave this table just as it is, only putting on more places, and serve lunch for some ladies here? Serve the same menu we have had. Marion, you call them up, and give the invitation. I'll 'phone to Chapman to let them off together. He can put two or three people there for an hour while they are gone, I'm sure. Tell them to take the roses with them."

Marion's eyes shone with her delight. He stood for a moment watching her before he went into the office to another telephone. It was one of the greatest pleasures the girl had ever had thus to pass on her beautiful time to those who had no part in it.

"Is that you, Gladys?" she said. She had chosen her first friend in the store to give the invitations. She knew what pleasure it would give her to convey it to the rest.

"This is Marion Warren"—she paused, and remembered that was no longer her name. "This *was* Marion Warren," she corrected, laughing. "I want to invite you girls at the counter to take lunch at the B_____ to-day. I am sorry not to be able to be here and receive you, but we are going right away. Mr. Lyman has telephoned to Mr. Chapman about allowing you all to go together for once, and you are to take the roses on the table when you leave. Divide them among you."

"Gee! Is that straight goods Marr—I mean Mrs. Lyman? You're just fooling, aren't you? Well, there's some class to that invite. Come? Course we will, every last one of us. Say, you're a real lady; do you know it? You're the bee's knees! Gee, I wish I could think of some way to let you know how much we all like this. When you get back, we'll come and see you, and tell you about it."

Marion turned to greet her husband with a laughing face but eyes in which the tears were very near. She knew just how much those girls would enjoy that. She had been one of them.

"Will he let them go?" she asked anxiously.

"Yes," said Lyman. "He demurred at first, wanted them to go in relays; but I held out, and told him he must for our wedding celebration; and he finally said he would. He said tell you he would put Miss Phipps and Jennie and Maria in charge, and you would know that things would go all right."

They were like two children playing with new toys, this happy bride and groom.

With a few directions to the head waiter about the luncheon they were giving they went on their way; and now, when they came out to the car, it had somehow been metamorphosed. It no longer had a little glass room behind, with a stately chauffeur's seat in front. Its roof had been folded back; its glass doors disappeared entirely somewhere; and it was just an open car with two seats, the back one of which was covered with roses. Marion was put in the front seat and Lyman got in beside her. The chauffeur stood smiling on the sidewalk.

"All right, Terence. You have the directions and the address. Very well, that's all. You put in the suitcases? Well, we'll meet you in New York sometime this afternoon if all goes well. Good-by."

Then the fine machinery of the car responded to its master's touch, and moved smoothly off down the street, leaving the respectful chauffeur bowing and smiling on the sidewalk.

"Why!" said Marion when she could get her breath from amazement, "is this car yours?"

"It is *ours*," he said with tender emphasis.

"Oh!" said Marion. "Oh! It is so wonderful! How can I ever get used to it?" After a moment's silence, in which her husband carefully guided his car through a tangle of moving vehicles and turned into a quieter street; "Oh, I suppose heaven will be like this. There will be so much, and all ours! and we won't know how to adjust ourselves to it all, not right at first."

"Dear child!" said Lyman, giving her a look of almost worship. "Does this seem that way to you? You make me feel humble. I never felt that I had so much. Perhaps you will teach me to be more thankful."

It was a wonderful trip to the two. Spring skies and gay little scurrying spring clouds overhead; in the distance soft purple hazels touched by tender green willows were coming into spring attire; now and then a woodsy space, with pink spring-beauties, or starred with hepatica and bloodroot, and a smell of earth and moist-growing things all about. Birds were hurrying about to secure the best locations, and everything in nature seemed joyous and happy.

To the girl who had never been outside her own city farther than the suburbs or some near-by woodland park on a picnic the whole experience was wonderful, of course; but the greatest thing of all was to keep realizing that the man beside her was her husband, and that she was to be privileged to stay beside him as long as they both should live. It seemed too wonderful to be true.

There followed long, delightful days of sightseeing and shopping in New York, when Marion felt that at last she was realizing her heart's desire and beginning to see and know "things," as she had often expressed it to herself in her lonely meditations.

Then one bright morning the chauffeur, who had seemed always to know just when to appear and take the car, brought it to the hotel door; and they started up to the Vermont farm to visit Tom and Jennie and the children.

Marion had carefully considered the idea of inviting at least Tom to the wedding, but decided against it. There would be so many endless explanations, perhaps wranglings and delays. Tom might object. Why worry him until it was all done, and he could see for himself what a wonderful brother-in-law he had acquired?

Packed carefully in the ample storage of the car were gifts. A new dress for Jennie, ready-made in a style that Marion knew would please her; a hat that she would consider a dream; gloves; and a number of other dainty feminine articles which Marion's experience with Jennie made her sure would be welcome; all sorts of pretty wearable and usable things for the children, besides a wonderful doll that could talk, and an Irish mail, and a bicycle. For Tom a fine watch; several pictures carefully selected with a view to interesting and uplifting the whole family; some of the latest books on scientific farming, and a large, beautiful reading-lamp. Marion was anxious that a little of her delight in higher things should reach these who were nearest to her in the world.

Lyman had seemed to enjoy the selection of these gifts as much as his wife did, and was helpful with suggestions. He seemed to understand at once all about Tom and Jennie, and to accept them as they were, and not expect any great things of them. Gradually Marion's fear of having them meet was wearing off. She began to understand that the true gentleman was always ready to see the true

172

man, no matter how rough an exterior; and Tom was not so rough as he might have been. He had a little touch of his father in him with all his disappointing qualities.

The chauffeur had been sent back home, and they took this trip alone. Lyman seemed to realize that his wife wanted no alien eye to witness the meeting between her husband and her brother, and with fine perception he made the way as easy for her as possible.

It was a great morning at the farm when they arrived.

Marion had written her brother of her coming marriage, but only in time for him to receive the letter a few hours before the ceremony. He could not have written her in time, and was little likely to telegraph about a matter of that sort. She had said in the letter that she and Lyman were going to Boston, and they might find it possible to stop over for a few hours and see them all; but nothing definite had been arranged.

So Tom and Jennie were in a state of sulkiness over the ingratitude of Marion. Jennie especially was out of humor about it. Marion was missed more and more. Jennie found it impossible to get hired help who could take her place. And now she had gone and got married! That was the end of it. But no; that might not be the end of it, either. Perhaps this new brother-in-law thought it would be a good thing to settle down upon them and take things easy. It might be that they would have Marion and her husband to look after now. Jennie suggested this snappishly that morning just after breakfast, but Tom only sighed and said:

"Yes, I don't suppose she's got anyone worthy of her. She was always so trustful of people, and she never had any business caution about her. I ought to have stayed in the city and looked after her."

"Nonsense!" said Jennie sharply. "She isn't a babe in arms, and you couldn't look after her. She would have her own way. It isn't your fault. And getting married isn't a business, either. But, if I were you, I'd make her understand plainly that he can't stay here long loafing on us, unless he turns to and helps in the planting. We can't afford to have him. He's most likely a lazy good-for-nothing——"

It was just at that moment that the eldest child called from the front door-step:

"Ma, oh Ma, there's a naughtymobile stopping at our big gate!"

"It's just someone wanting to know the way to the village, I suppose," said Jennie discontentedly, hurrying, nevertheless, to the door to look out. "Tom, you go down and tell them. I'm sure I don't see why people can't read the sign-posts."

Then almost instantly her voice changed.

"Tom, they've opened the big gate, and are coming in. You go out and see who it is, for pity's sake, while I take down my curl-papers. Goodness! Suppose they should want to come in and rest, and the spare room not finished yet. I washed the curtains yesterday, but they're lying on the bed. If it's tourists to stay, we'll put them in the parlour; and you'll have to come up and help me put the curtains up quick."

Jennie's tongue went no faster than her hands. The curl-papers were out of sight in a twinkling, and her coiffure settled into its company aspect. Three aprons, a rubber doll, and a little sunbonnet were swept into a closet with one movement; and the hall table received a swift dusting with the apron she wore, while it was yet in process of being snatched off to share the seclusion of the other three. Then a chorused shout from the children outside the door made her pause and listen.

"Aunt Marion! It's Aunt Marion!" they warbled gleefully and Jennie's hasty preparations relaxed into grim dignity.

But how in the world did Marion come to arrive in such a fine automobile? This was her first thought. Very likely they had lost their way, and some kind chauffeur had offered to give them a lift in their long walk. If it had been a farm-wagon, now, that would have been quite likely; but chauffeurs and automobile-owners, what few of them there were about that neighborhood, were not wont to be so kindly. However, that was probably the explanation.

It was to be hoped that neither Marion nor her good-for-nothing husband had met with an accident such as a sprained or broken ankle or leg, which made it necessary for even the iron heart of a limousine to relent and pause for them. A broken leg would be an excellent reason for living at the farm gratis for several weeks. Jennie had set her lips firmly. If anyone had broken a leg, he could go to the hospital in the village. There were excellent nurses and a good doctor there. She, Jennie, had no time or strength to wait on invalids.

With this thought she went out to greet her unwelcome guests.

Chapter XVIII

THE CAR STOOD IN FRONT of the great flat stone by the side door, and a tall, handsome man with a long fur-lined coat was helping a lady out. Jennie hurriedly glanced about; but, not seeing any other travellers, concluded the children had made a mistake, and brought her eyes back to the lady.

Marion wore a long fur coat also, for the air in that northern climate was still cold for a long drive. Jennie's discerning eyes made out that the coat was real mink and that the crimson roses she was wearing were not artificial, even before her eyes rested on the face beneath the becoming hat. The three children surrounded the newcomer, climbing upon her as if she were their long-lost property, regardless of mink and roses. Jennie started forward in horror to reprove them; but Marion, having stooped to kiss the baby, lifted laughing eyes to greet her sister-in-law, and Jennie suddenly recognized her.

"Why, Marion Warren! What on earth?" she exclaimed, starting back. Then Tom came to the front. Men take astonishing things with less surprise. He had grasped the fact of his sister's bettered condition like a flash as he stood watching the car drive into the yard. His practised eye knew at once that it was a private car and that the man who sat beside his sister was no hanger-on who could be put to work in the hay-field if he lingered too long for convenience. By the time the car stopped at the door he was ready with a hearty greeting for both his sister and her husband, and he already felt on intimate terms with his new brother-in-law; for Lyman's hearty grasp and pleasant smile had won his frank, open-hearted nature at once.

"Jennie, this is Marion's husband, Mr. Lyman. Lyman,

this is my wife," he said loudly. "Jennie, why don't you open the door and let these travellers in? I know they are tired and cold. Nannie, let go of your Aunt Marion's hand. Don't you see you are crowding her off the step? Come, children; get out of the way. Run into the house, and get some chairs ready for them to sit on."

Tom's loud tone of deference showed Jennie that the new brother-in-law had made an impression on her husband already. Not so easily convinced herself, she looked at Lyman sharply, and was somewhat abashed to meet his pleasant gaze and to see the twinkle in his eye. Her face suddenly grew very red at the remembrance of what she had said about putting this new relative to work planting potatoes. She perceived at once that he would be as much out of place at that occupation as a silk gown on washday. But it was characteristic of Jennie that it vexed her to be taken by surprise. Although she had pictured a most undesirable brother-in-law, whose advent could but bring trouble and dissension to their home, she was annoyed that it had turned out otherwise than her prophecy, so that it was with an ill grace that she shook hands stiffly with Lyman, and preceded him into the house, where she felt quite ill at ease. How was she to manage for this grand company with no one to help her? One could scarcely expect such a dressed-up minx of a Marion to help get dinner. It was just as she had expected, after all. Marion had arranged things so that she would have everything easy, and be a lady living on her brother's wife. She looked belligerently at the bride, who was surrounded again by the three adoring children, being divested of fur coat and chic hat and roses as fast as six little hands could accomplish it. Tom beamed joyously over the whole, and loudly told his new brother-in-law to make himself at home at once. There seemed no place in the whole setting for the ill-used Jennie.

It was Marion whose keen eyes saw and understood, and, freeing herself from the little detaining hands, arose.

"Come, Jennie," she cried; "get me an apron, and I'll help get dinner. It was mean of us to come down upon you this way without a warning, but we were not quite sure whether we could get here so early; and, besides, I did enjoy surprising you so much. What a lovely big house this is! I'm in a great hurry to see the whole of it. Is this

177

the way to the kitchen? Come on, and get me an apron."

Jennie somewhat mollified by the offer of help, followed her, protesting stiffly that she must not think of helping, but relieved, nevertheless, and more than curious about the bride's attire, her husband, and, most of all, the car in which they had come.

"Where did you get it?" she demanded as soon as they reached the kitchen, her eyes meanwhile travelling over the bride's costume with comprehensive glance and resting scrutinizingly on the diamond which now guarded Marion's wedding-ring.

Marion, smiling, held out her hand.

"My ring, do you mean?" she said pleasantly. "Isn't it beautiful? I never expected to have even the tiniest diamond, and to have this great beauty was wonderful. I was so surprised when he gave it to me."

"No, I didn't mean that," said Jennie bluntly. "I hadn't noticed that yet, though it's big enough to see a mile off, goodness knows. Is it real?"

Marion felt indignant, but she managed to say, "Yes," very gently, though she withdrew her hand from inspection. It seemed to desecrate her new joy to have unsympathetic eyes and tongue at work upon it. Perhaps pretty soon Jennie would ask whether Lyman's love was genuine. She probably would if it occurred to her to do so. Marion shrank from the ordeal.

"It must have cost a lot of money if it's real. In my opinion people better put their money away for a rainy day than to flaunt it in gewgaws, but tastes differ. As for me, I never expect to have even a paste diamond. Though I don't know but it's a good thing he gave it to you. If you ever get in need, you could sell it."

"Jennie!" Marion could not keep the horror from her voice.

"Well, it's just as well to think of those things. You never know how a marriage is going to turn out. Are you sure he's all right? Where'd you meet him, anyway?"

Marion controlled her feelings, although her cheeks were very red, and answered gently:

"Mr. Radnor introduced us at a church social."

"Well, it's plain to be seen why you married him," grudged Jennie. "You always did like pretty things and pretty people, and he certainly isn't bad-looking. And you

178

seem to have blossomed out in stylish clothes on the strength of it. I hope you had the money to pay for them."

"They are all paid for," said Marion quietly.

"H'm!" said Jennie. "They must have cost a lot. But what I was asking you about at first was the automobile. Where did you get it? Did you hire it in the village? I didn't know they had them to hire in the village."

Marion smiled.

"Oh, no. It is our car," she said. "We came all the way from New York since yesterday morning in it. The ride was beautiful. I have enjoyed the trip so much——"

"Your car!" interrupted Jennie. "What on earth do you mean, Marion Warren? Are you telling me the truth?"

"I certainly am," said Marion, laughing now at the comical expression of her sister-in-law's face. "Come, Jennie; let's hurry and get dinner; for I've brought a few things for the children, and I want to open them. Is Nannie as fond of dolls as ever?"

"Are you sure it's paid for, Marion?" asked Jennie anxiously. "They say hardly anybody that owns an automobile pays for it. They say they just mortgage their houses to get them, or go in debt. You can't be sure about anybody."

"Well, you needn't worry, Jennie. This is all paid for, and my husband has money enough left to make us entirely comfortable. Come, Jennie, where is an apron? Were you going to peel these potatoes? Let me do them."

"Marion Warren, have you married a real rich man? Tell me at once."

"I suppose I have," answered the bride meekly with a dimple in each cheek. "I never understood how it happened, but it's true."

"Well, then you can go right out of this kitchen. I'm not going to have a rich sister-in-law peeling potatoes for dinner in my kitchen. I know what is fitting if I am blunt in my speech."

"Nonsense, Jennie! I'm no different because my husband has a little money. I'm just the same girl I was a year ago."

"Indeed you're not!" said Jennie, taking the knife from her, and going at the potatoes furiously. "Look at your shoes and your dress, it looks as if a tailor made it. And you're wearing roses in the morning. If you've really got the money to pay for it all, why, you've a right to be waited on, I suppose. Anyhow, you're not going to sit down in that dress and peel potatoes in my kitchen. And wasn't that a real mink coat you wore? Goodness! It's a wonder you weren't ashamed to bring your fine husband up here."

In vain did Marion protest. Jennie would have none of her assistance. She worked rapidly, and soon had a good dinner in preparation. She brought forth her best preserves and pickles and the last of the fruit-cake she had been saving for the church sewing-society when it would meet with her the following week. Jennie was not so bad, after all, when she really was impressed, and she was impressed at last.

She went about with martyr-like attitude, treating Marion with a deferential stiffness that was as unpleasant as her former attitude had been. When Marion insisted upon setting the table, Jennie sent Nannie to perform the task, saying with a heavy sigh: "I have done my own work and set my own table for a good many years, and shall probably have to continue to do so all my life. One setting of a table more or less will make little difference. It's not with me as it is with you."

And this style of conversation continued until Marion was almost sorry she had come, and retreated at last to the parlor, which had been made delightful with a great open fire in the old-fashioned fireplace. Then Nannie forsook her table-setting, and nestled down close to her; and the other two children climbed into her lap, and demanded a story just where she had left off the year before. Lyman, talking politics to the delight of Tom, who had missed his city friends when it came to election-time, yet found time to watch his wife as she made a pretty picture of herself with the little ones about her.

The dinner would have been a trying affair with Jennie sitting up straight and stiff and dispensing her hospitalities without a smile, and Marion shy and embarrassed, wondering what her husband would think of it all, if it had not been for Lyman, who adapted himself to the situation with the most charming simplicity, talking intimately with Tom about the farm, admiring the view from the windows, discussing the possibilities of crops, then turning to the children with the story of a little dog they saw on the way, and even bringing a softened expression to Jennie's mouth when he admired her plum jam.

Marion watched him with growing pride and love, and Jennie watched her surreptitiously, and marvelled. What a lady she had become! Did a few costly garments make all the difference there was between them, or had it been there all the time? These were the thoughts that were troubling Jennie.

As soon as dinner was over, Marion coaxed them all into the parlor, and Lyman brought the things from the car into the room. Thinking the gifts were all for the children, the father and mother gathered eagerly around to watch them untied. Jennie had thawed in her manner somewhat, but was not yet altogether cordial. She sat stiffly in one of the parlor chairs, and watched Nannie's eager fingers untie the cord of a large box; and then suddenly the child threw back the lid of the box and screamed with delight over the beautiful doll. The mother's face relaxed then into real pleasure as she saw the costly doll and her little girl's delight. Tom entered into the excitement as if he had been a boy, and helped the two little boys undo their packages, even shouting with them over what they brought to light, and beginning at once to set up the little electric railway that the new uncle had brought them.

In the midst of the tumult Marion brought the hat-box, and the suit-box, and the packages containing the other things she had for Jennie, around to the couch, and motioned her sister-in-law to come to her. Thinking these were more things for the children, and thoroughly mollified now, Jennie came, and helped with untying the strings. When she saw the beautiful dress, and understood that it was for herself, her face was a study of conflicting emotions; amazement, doubt, shame, and delight contended for the mastery.

"Do you like it?" asked Marion. "If you would rather have something else, I think I could change it on my way back and send it to you."

Jennie laid eager hands on the soft silken material, and smoothed it lovingly.

"Well, I should think I did like it," said Jennie, at last melted out of her frigidity. "I never expected to have anything half so fine; and the color is just what I always wanted, and never could seem to find except in expensive stuff. I'm sure I'm very much obliged to you, Marion."

"Oh, I'm so glad you like it!" said Marion, pleased; "and I do hope it fits you. I tried it on; but I used to be smaller than you, and I wasn't sure it would fit you. It was large for me."

"Oh, I'm sure it'll fit. It looks good and large. I'm just glad to have it made; for the dressmaker out here isn't very good and they never see anything as stylish as this. I'm real pleased."

But, when Marion opened the hat-box, and brought forth the hat, graceful and simple in its lines, yet beautiful, and bearing that unmistakable stamp of the lady, Jennie succumbed entirely. It was the last straw that broke her barriers down. She looked and looked, and could say nothing, and then looked again as Marion set it on her own head.

Then Marion put the hat on Jennie, and sent her to the glass to see; and Jennie walked solemnly from the room, her kitchen apron still tied about her waist, but her head borne regally, mindful of its crowning glory. Tom and Lyman stopped talking, and Tom shouted out his hearty approval, till his wife's face grew rosy with pleasure. She stayed a long time in the guest room before the looking-glass; and Marion, fearful lest she did not like the hat, followed shyly, and found her looking at herself intently in the glass, and two great tears rolling down her flushed cheeks.

"Don't you like it, Jennie?" she asked anxiously.

"Like it!" said Jennie, turning full upon her. "I like it better than anything I ever had in my life before, and I don't deserve it. I've been awful mean to you sometimes, and I've almost hated you because you didn't come up here and help us get settled, and because you always held yourself away from things, and seemed to think nothing was good enough for you; but I'm ashamed now, and I oughtn't to take these nice things. They don't belong to me, and I don't deserve to have you bring such nice presents to me nor the children. I'm sorry, and I ask you to forgive me."

And suddenly Jennie, the grim and forbidding, burst into tears, and fell upon her astonished sister-in-law's neck. But Marion's loving heart was equal to the occasion. With abounding forgiveness she received Jennie's overture and folded her arms lovingly about her, rejoicing that at last she had won her sister.

"But you don't know it all yet," sobbed out Jennie lifting her head from Marion's shoulder. "You'll never forgive me but I've got to tell. I can't sleep nights thinking of it. I stole your father's will and hid it so it wouldn't be found. I didn't destroy it, but I hid it, so you'd never know the house was all yours. And now I can't find the will anymore, it's gone."

Marion's hand rested softly on Jennie's head. Marion's voice was very gentle as she said: "That's all right, Jennie. I forgave it long ago."

Jennie lifted her astonished head and stared:

"You forgave it? Then you knew it?"

"Yes, I knew it. The will fell out from behind the desk when the movers were carrying it out of the house."

"But you didn't know *I* did it."

"Yes, Jennie, you had dropped a bit of your peppermint candy into the envelope. I knew it must have been you. But it's all right now. I burned it up. Let's forget it. I've got something far better than the old house. You must come and see me in my new one."

"You knew I'd done it and yet you forgave me!" marvelled Jennie. "And you never *told*, either! You're an angel, Marion Warren, and I'm a devil. But I'll love you always, and I'll do anything in the world for you. We'll sell this farm and give you back your money. Tom hasn't been happy about it either, but he didn't know what I'd done."

"You will not sell this farm, Jennie dear, and Tom is *never* to know about that will. I don't want the money and I *do* want you to have the farm. I've more money than I know how to spend, so please, please forget it, I have, and let us have a good time!"

They came into the other room in a few minutes with shining faces.

"We may as well open the rest of these things," said Lyman, producing the packages meant for Tom; and Tom, nothing loath, and unsuspecting, took the small box handed him, and presently found the fine watch, and the books and other things; and the two sat down and had a real brotherly chat over the good cheer that had been brought.

Lyman, as he watched the brother, caught little gleams of resemblance to his wife in the rougher, heartier features; little tricks of speech and mannerisms that were pleasant to recognize; and he saw at once that the brother was no blockhead. He might not care for music and art and philosophy; but he would make a keen business man, and was a good talker. His arguments in politics were well put and the points sharp and original. He might be of far coarser mould than his fair and delicate sister; but there was nothing about him to be ashamed of, and the new brother-in-law was enjoying himself immensely.

Finally Lyman and Tom went out to look over the farm while Marion and Jennie cleared off the table, and there was no more talk about rich and poor, for there was a final truce between Jennie and Marion.

They rode away the next morning into a sunlit world, having left happy hearts and pleasant feelings behind them, and really sorry that it was not possible to have planned to accept the urgent invitations of both host and hostess to remain a few days longer. How they would have shouted with merriment if they could have known how Jennie feared they were coming to live on them, and of her plans to put her new brother-in-law to work on the farm to earn his board!

But, as they waved a good-by to the group on the side porch, and turned into the broad highway with the prospect of a glorious spring day before them, and just their two selves in all the great, beautiful world, Lyman felt that now indeed his bride belonged to him entirely. Until he had seen her people he knew she felt ill at ease with him whenever she thought of the wide difference in their birth. But he had somehow managed to make it plain to her that all the world is kin, and that he felt no such gulf as she had feared. He could see that her heart was light from the burden lifted, and now she felt that she might rest in his love and be happy.

Also there was a feeling of exhilaration upon them both, for they had won a victory over Jennie, and made her their devoted admirer. It gave Marion a great sense of peace to know this. Jennie might not be any pleasanter for daily living than before, when the newness wore off; but she did not have to live with her, and it was good to know that Jennie bore no grudges. Marion enjoyed thinking of the pleasant surprises she would send them all, and so make up to Jennie for any fancied wrongs of the past. So Marion sat beside her husband, happy and smiling, as they flew along the great wide road, and drew in the morning breath of spring sweetness, and delighted in the glance of each other's eyes.

At New York they found the chauffeur and a lot of letters.

Lyman had taken care to have announcement cards sent to all their friends before they left home, and now the congratulations were pouring down upon them. Marion gasped as she opened one exquisitely perfumed epistle written in exceedingly tall chirography on the latest mode of paper with a gold embossed monogram.

"You dear little Marion;" it began familiarly.

"How you have stolen a march upon us all! Though I'll tell you a secret. I suspected long ago what was going on, and have been perfectly delighted over the prospect; but I didn't tell a soul. Wasn't I good?

"I am charmed that you are to enter our circle and be one of us. It is a real pleasure to think of you as mistress of that lovely home. I shall be so pleased to be 'near neighbors' and run in often. I have always admired you greatly, and wanted to see more of you, and have often grieved over the separation that circumstances made necessary as we grew older. And now you are coming right into our set, and there will be nothing to hinder our being bosom friends. Your husband and I have always been very intimate, and so I have a double claim upon you, you see; and I do hope my note will be the first you receive to tell you how glad we all are to have you among us. I intend to give a large dinner for you just as soon as you are settled at home and ready for your social duties.

"It is not necessary for me to tell you what a wonderful husband you have married, for you probably know that. Tell him for me that he is to be congratulated upon the bride he has chosen."

"Yours always lovingly,

"ISABEL CRESSON."

The gift that came with the note was a paperweight

185

of green jade in the form of an exquisitely carved little idol with a countenance like a Chinese devil.

"Oh!" gasped Marion, helplessly letting the note slip from her fingers to the floor. "Oh!"

"What is the matter, dear?" asked Lyman, turning from a letter from a business friend.

"Oh!" said Marion. "I am ashamed to have misjudged her so. She is very kind, I'm sure; but—but—I don't think I shall ever really quite enjoy her, she's such an awful hypocrite. I shall always think of her in that gold dress!"

Lyman picked up the letter, and read it with growing amusement.

"Don't worry, dear," he said, laughing. "This is just what I've expected, and you've yet to learn that this young woman can be several very different people. It suits her just now to pose as my intimate friend—and yours. But no one is thereby deceived. Everyone of our circle knows that she has always been my special aversion. There are reasons why she will never be likely to say any disagreeable things to you, and you need not fear her; but, as for making her your intimate friend, that will never be necessary. Be your own sweet self, gracious and simple to her; but never let her deceive you into thinking you are wrong in your own intuition about her. She has no right to claim even toleration from you. She is a cruel, selfish, rotten-hearted woman. She is simply showing you that she is robbed of her power to hurt you, and prefers to make the best of it, and be as intimate as you will allow."

Two days after, they returned; and Marion entered the great, handsome house, and looked about upon the beauty and luxury which were henceforth to be hers. Everywhere, in all the rooms, there were roses to welcome her, great crimson roses, glowing in masses, in crystal bowls and jardinières, and costly vases. But on her dressing-table in the little white boudoir he had prepared for her, standing in a clear glass vase so that its long green stem was clearly seen, there nodded and glowed a single crimson bud.